T4-APU-712

A WATERY GRAVE

Ten pirates with drawn swords forced Zorro to the end of the plank. He hung suspended for a moment over the rushing waves, his hands tightly bound. His beloved Lolita, horrified as she watched from below, was unable to help him. The brave adventurer's fate was sealed.

"Give him to the sea!" Bardoso, the pirate captain, commanded.

"Zorro!" Lolita screamed.

The plank was tipped. With Lolita's cry ringing in his ears, Zorro dropped to the sea as if he were made of lead. In an instant he was gone.

Bantam Starfire Books of related interest
Ask your bookseller for the books you have missed

THE APE INSIDE ME by Kin Platt
THE BIG DEAL by Jack Glasgow
THE CRY OF THE SEALS by Larry Weinberg
DUNKER by Ronald Kidd
FINGERS by William Sleator
HOLLYWOOD DREAM MACHINE by Bonnie Zindel
IN THE WINGS by Katie Goldman
ISLE OF THE SHAPESHIFTERS by Otto Coontz
LITTLE LITTLE by M. E. Kerr
MAYBE NEXT YEAR . . . by Amy Hest
ON THAT DARK NIGHT by Carol Beach York
WAR ZONE by Larry Weinberg

Zorro

and the
PIRATE RAIDERS

by D. J. Arneson

as adapted from a story
by Johnston McCulley

BANTAM BOOKS
TORONTO · NEW YORK · LONDON · SYDNEY · AUCKLAND

RL 6, IL age 11 and up

ZORRO AND THE PIRATE RAIDERS

A Bantam Book / January 1986

Starfire and accompanying logo of a stylized star are registered trademarks of Bantam Books, Inc. Registered in U.S. Patent and Trademark Office and elsewhere.

All rights reserved.
Copyright © 1985 by Zorro Productions.
This book may not be reproduced in whole or in part, by mimeograph or any others means, without permission.
For information address: Bantam Books, Inc.

ISBN 0-553-24670-4

Published simultaneously in the United States and Canada

Bantam Books are published by Bantam Books, Inc. Its trademark, consisting of the words "Bantam Books" and the portrayal of a rooster, is Registered in U.S. Patent and Trademark Office and in other countries. Marca Registrada. Bantam Books, Inc., 666 Fifth Avenue, New York, New York 10103.

PRINTED IN THE UNITED STATES OF AMERICA

O   0 9 8 7 6 5 4 3 2 1

Zorro

and the
PIRATE RAIDERS

ONE

ᔔ

Land Rats and Water Rats

Black water hissed like a snake along the sides of the sinister ship as it sailed off the coast of southern California. It glided through a fog so thick the blazing overhead sun could not be seen.

By night, the dark ship quietly drifted less than a mile offshore, still enveloped in fog. Her smoky lanterns were extinguished to avoid detection.

It was a strange craft, foul and grim. Her paint was faded and chipped from months at sea. Her decks were littered with junk, but her sails and running gear were in perfect repair. A touch of her helm turned her bow like the nose of a shark fresh on a scent.

The fog parted and for an instant the ship's gray decks were bathed with the silver light of a brilliant moon. The figure of a man stood motionless at the rail. He was the ship's commander, the infamous Bardoso!

Bardoso was a giant man, as thick around the waist as a cannon, with tiny, piglike eyes set deep in a fierce face. Large gold rings hung from his mutilated ears.

Shirtless and barefoot, he stood staring toward the booming surf that marked the shore. He glanced to the topmost mast, and his grim face froze in anger. "Sanchez!" he roared in a voice that drowned out the sound of crashing waves. "Is it necessary to shout to the world our villainy? Look! The flag of the devil still flies."

Bardoso's lieutenant, Sanchez, a smaller version of his evil chief, leaped to the deck. His eyes followed Bardoso's fiery stare to the top of the mast. Flapping limply was the black-and-white skull and crossbones, which left no doubt what manner of ship Bardoso commanded.

Sanchez shouted at a nearby sailor who quickly lowered the telltale flag.

The black flag was no sooner lowered when the fog lifted like a curtain. The land, bathed in silver, lay before the ship, silent and unprotected.

Bardoso grasped his broad-bladed sword. "There," he said as he pointed toward shore with the tip of his Spanish steel cutlass. "We go ashore there, against the cliffs."

As if answering to his command, the ship glided toward a point of land protected by towering white cliffs. At the same time, eighty armed men climbed eagerly from the ship's dark hold. Their cutlasses flashed grimly in the pale moonlight.

Bardoso stepped to the rail nearest shore. "You and a small band of men will accompany me, Sanchez," he said. "The rest of the crew will stay with the ship. As soon as we are landed, they must put to sea to stand offshore until we return tomorrow night, exactly two hours before dawn."

"Sí, my chief, I have already given the order," Sanchez said.

Bardoso stroked his black beard. "It will be a pretty party, eh, Sanchez?" he said. "With loot enough for all. Food, wine, gold, precious jewels—and *more!*"

Sanchez wet his lips. A vision of chests full of treasure, tables laden with food, and beautiful prisoners passed before his narrowed eyes. "A banquet of treasure!" he exclaimed. "And none too soon."

Bardoso nodded. "Too true, Sanchez. We have sailed up and down this paltry coast for four months with nothing to show for our raids but a few pigs and cows. But now we are ready for my boldest raid—"

"It is arranged?" Sanchez asked, daring to question Bardoso to his face. It was a feat no other man would risk if he cared for his life.

Bardoso's mouth flashed open, baring yellow teeth against bloodred lips. "Señor Pirate, do you take me for a fool to rush in where things are not properly arranged? If so, then you must face the consequences of thinking me a fool." Bardoso patted the handle of his sword. It was not a menacing gesture, but Sanchez understood well its intent.

"I would never call you such," Sanchez said. "To your face."

Bardoso's eyes narrowed. He and Sanchez understood one another. Each trusted the other the way beasts of prey do as they circle a prize big enough for only one of them.

Bardoso put his face close to that of his chief henchman. "I will tell you how well arranged this raid is, Sanchez," he said. He glanced over his shoulder. The armed landing party sat impatiently in bobbing longboats alongside the pirate ship. He turned back to Sanchez. "The governor's own man has arranged this raid for us."

Bardoso's head flew back, and a raucous laugh roared from the depths of his throat. "What a pre-

cious pair of scoundrels," he said. "The governor
and his man may be caballeros, rich men of the
upper class, but the blood that flows in their veins
is as villainous as any you'll find spilled when a pirate is split by Spanish steel."

Sanchez understood what his chief meant. Their
raid was approved and planned by the very man
who was sworn to protect the people from pirates.
His eyes darted back and forth. "I don't like it," he
said. "It appears too easy. It could be a trap—"

Bardoso drew his huge sword and smashed it flat
side down against the rail.

Sanchez leaped clear of the flashing blade. He
knew it was only a gesture, but he also knew his
chief made no gestures he did not mean.

"Don't speak of treachery or traps to me," Bardoso bellowed. "Have your heart and mind gone
soft? Or do you believe I am one to fall into a trap?"
He raised the point of his sword to Sanchez's
throat. "If that is what you think, then I wonder why I
don't feed you to the sharks."

Sanchez held his ground, but he did not move for
his sword.

Slowly, Bardoso withdrew his sword, and then
lowered himself into the first boat. "You will do well
to let me plan the details of our business, Sanchez.
Now let us get on."

With a nod from Bardoso, the pirates' brawny
arms dipped their oars into the black water and began to pull for land. The small craft were soon clear
of the towering pirate ship.

Bardoso searched the shoreline with eyes trained
to see what others might miss. He leaned forward
so his men could hear as he whispered, "Silence,
you devils. We have nothing to fear unless you announce our presence to some poor fool on those

shores. Our raids in these parts have made us detested, and many would leap at the chance to warn our enemies of our coming." Then he added with a low laugh, "But if it is noise you want, you'll have your fill tomorrow night when we take our prize."

Sanchez studied Bardoso from his perch in the tossing boat. He understands the men well, he thought. He knows they despise a journey over land, but each time he hints of the treasures that await them, they forget their fears and they follow.

The boats soon landed beneath the shelter of a low cliff, and the men scurried ashore to stand in a nervous circle around Bardoso. They watched as the small boats returned to their ship. Once aboard, the skeleton crew raised sails and turned the ghostlike pirate craft toward the open sea. Within minutes it vanished into the thick fog.

The thought that the ship might not return for them crossed the mind of every pirate left onshore.

Bardoso defiantly turned his back on his ship as he unfolded a small, crudely drawn map. Holding it so its inked lines matched the contours of the shore and the dark canyon, he gestured to Sanchez. "Forward," he said. "And warn these scoundrels that any noise is a request for the point of my sword."

With Sanchez at his side and the restless crew following, Bardoso turned toward the canyon and began the long march toward their goal—the rich settlement of Reina de los Angeles. "Give no quarter to anyone who crosses our path," the pirate chief ordered. "We must arrive in secrecy."

His lieutenant grinned. "Pity the merchant or brown-frocked friar who stumbles our way."

Bardoso spun on the sand and grabbed Sanchez's arm in a grip so tight the stunned man thought his bones would be crushed. "You'll harm no friar!" he hissed.

Sanchez pulled back, trying not to look shaken. "Have you suddenly begun to love the robes and gowns of the missionaries?" he asked.

"I love to protect myself in any way I can," Bardoso replied. "It is better to avoid trouble than to seek it." His muscles quivered as he paused in his speech. "I knew a man who once struck a friar," he whispered. "I would wish his fate on no one." Then, without further explanation, he marched on.

A stream coursed through the floor of the canyon. The pirates followed it mile after mile toward the distant, sleeping town that few of them other than Bardoso and Sanchez had ever seen.

The pirates didn't voice their fears, but they wondered to themselves what had happened to make this bold adventure safe when earlier, such an enterprise would have been considered foolhardy—or fatal. So far their chief had told them nothing to calm their curiosity.

By dawn the dread crew was within easy striking distance of the town. Bardoso led his men to the safety of a cave where they could spend the day resting. They would need their strength when once again the moon rose.

As the march-weary men tossed in fitful sleep on the unfamiliar ground, Bardoso signaled for Sanchez to join him. He spread his parchment map on the earth and put his finger on the X, which marked the edge of town just over the next set of hills. "We may have to split into two groups," he whispered. "You will command one. Therefore, you should know more about this business."

"I'm listening," Sanchez replied.

"A high official will meet us at the edge of town tomorrow night," Bardoso said.

Sanchez glanced at the map. Though it was crudely drawn, he could read it well. "I have heard you call him 'the governor's man,'" he said. "How can we trust him?"

"Because he *is* the governor's man," Bardoso spat back.

Sanchez's brow furrowed. "All the more reason for a pirate band to distrust him, no?"

Bardoso grinned. "Reina de los Angeles will be wide open to us, my friend, because we have an unknown benefactor who has caused the governor to close his eyes to the likes of us.

"Things have changed since the last time we visited Reina de los Angeles," Bardoso continued. "The governor of the lands of California, who has his palatial estate in San Francisco Asís, has an enemy in Reina de los Angeles he wishes to punish."

"He must hate him terribly to invite pirates to do his work," Sanchez said.

Bardoso scowled. "The governor, as you know, has his way with the people he is sworn to protect. His officials steal what they want from them—in the name of the law."

Sanchez grinned. "I know," he said. "They are pirates like us, but they have the protection of the governor who in turn benefits from their allegiance to him."

"Exactly," Bardoso said. "But a righteous caballero now threatens to unsettle their tidy arrangement. The governor learned of him on a recent trip south to Reina de los Angeles."

Sanchez spat into the dirt. "A caballero?" he said sharply. "What do governors or pirates have to fear from satin-caped gentlemen, dressed in finery, who parade in the sun on blooded horses and practice what passes for swordsmanship on straw dummies that can't fight back?"

"Perhaps nothing," Bardoso said with a hint of uncertainty in his voice. "But there is one such who has set the governor to trembling. He is a high-wayman who—"

Risking a thick fist across his mouth, Sanchez leaned forward in disbelief. "A highwayman? But you said a gentleman."

"Silence, and let me finish!" Bardoso snapped. "This enemy of the governor is a gentleman *and* a highwayman. But unlike our true brothers on land who steal for themselves, this scoundrel has made it his duty to protect the weak and innocent. He and his elegant friends seek to punish the officials who rob and cheat the people with the governor's bless-ing."

"Ho, ho!" Sanchez laughed. "What irony. But why doesn't the governor dispense with this foppish fly?"

Bardoso's face grew dark. "Because this 'foppish fly,' as you call him, is a man who, if we had a dozen of him in our company, would give us the courage and strength to raid all of Mexico, the entire Span-ish fleet, and attack the whole of Europe as well."

"No man is that bold," Sanchez said.

Bardoso merely nodded. "This man is. With his mark he has struck fear in the governor's heart like no other."

"His mark?" Sanchez asked curiously. "What is that?"

Bardoso traced the blunt end of a thick finger through the dust of the cave floor, a ragged slash which formed the familiar letter Z.

"A Z?" Sanchez said. "His mark is a Z and people fear it?" He could not believe what Bardoso was telling him. "Then they would surely run at the sight of an X, or an A—"

Bardoso grabbed Sanchez by his tattered shirt and pulled him close. "It is not the mark that strikes fear, you fool, but the manner in which it is left. With swordsmanship that leaves men breathless, this righteous highwayman engraves his victims with his mark."

Before Sanchez could raise a hand to protect himself, Bardoso traced a dusty Z across his forehead. "It is the Mark of Zorro that turns the governor's heart to jelly," he hissed.

Sanchez wiped the mark from his head. "Zorro? The *Fox*? That is his name?"

"That is how he calls himself," Bardoso said. "Whoever he is, when the governor visited Reina de los Angeles, this righteous land pirate told him in no uncertain terms to return to San Francisco and never return. He even told the governor to abdicate his position, which he did not do, of course."

"But where do we fit in?" Sanchez asked, more puzzled than ever.

"The governor seeks to punish Reina de los Angeles for harboring this Zorro in its midst," Bardoso said.

"Ah!" Sanchez said, beginning to see the devious plan for himself. "By looking the other way while we raid Reina de los Angeles, the town will be punished."

"You are worthy to be my second in command, Sanchez," Bardoso said, giving his lieutenant rare praise. "That is precisely it. The governor's man provides us with the information and protection we need to make our raid, while the governor himself sends his troops racing up and down the coast as if looking for us." Now Bardoso chuckled. "The governor will seem to be protecting the town as is his duty, and we will be safe."

"With the loot," Sanchez added.

Bardoso scowled. "With half the loot. The other half goes to the governor's man for his part."

Sanchez scratched his beard knowingly. "Of course," he said. Then he quickly added, "But why not keep it all?"

Bardoso shook his huge head. "Beneath it all you are still the fool," he said. "Don't you see if we work with the governor in this matter, we'll snare him in our net and all the rich towns of his domain will be ours?"

Sanchez didn't reply. He understood. They were all pirates bound by the perverse honor of thieves where every man's back was a fair target for the dagger of the other.

The plan to raid Reina de los Angeles was simple. The governor's man would see to it the soldiers of the garrison guarding the town would not interfere. He would provide horses for the pirate band to flee on, and as many carts as needed to carry off the loot.

At nightfall, Bardoso raised his men. They gathered silently around him and at his signal, followed him through the darkness. They soon reached the crest of a small hill. On the other side flickered the fires and lamps of Reina de los Angeles.

As the men waited, Bardoso and Sanchez crawled forward, their bellies pressed tight against the ground, to a better vantage place above the town.

Many simple houses dotted the dim landscape. Beyond them, large and elegant in the pale light of the moon, stood the rich mansions of the high-ranking, wealthy citizens. To the right was the garrison that housed the soldiers, and on the left was the church.

The two pirates got slowly to their feet and carefully followed the shadows down the hill until they stood within a musket shot of the town. There they waited impatiently for the governor's man to appear.

"Psst!"

The sound from deep in the darkness caused both pirates to draw their cutlasses, but the noise was quickly followed by a password agreed to earlier.

A figure draped in a long, dark cloak stepped from the shadows. "Where are your men?" he asked.

"They are ready," Bardoso replied, unwilling to divulge more than he had to lest the traitor prove even more treacherous than the plan.

"Good," the man said. "It will be best for them to strike in an hour. The way will be clear. The soldiers will be sent in the opposite direction on a wild-goose chase, and the town will be yours."

"And you?" Bardoso asked.

"I will absent myself to remain above suspicion," the man said. "Once you have done your work and have your loot, return at once to the sea. The soldiers will be sent on another misdirected chase, and you will be safe."

Bardoso smiled at the plan. "Good," he said. "We will strike as soon as they are gone."

The man in the dark cape then inched close to the huge pirate chief. "There is one other thing I will ask," he said. "It is a personal favor to me. My share of the loot, you could say."

Bardoso's tone was suspicious. "We agreed to no favors," he said. "But speak."

The man grinned evilly. "It is the matter of taking a prisoner for me," he said. "A woman. The señorita Lolita Pulido, daughter of Don Carlos Pulido, an enemy of the governor. She is to be my prize for this adventure. I wish her to be seized and taken unharmed to your ship. I will meet you at a safe rendezvous far down the coast in four or five days to claim her. And be assured, señor pirate, the governor will not mind this abduction."

Bardoso shrugged. "As you will. It is all the same to me."

The cloaked man grew bold. "One more thing, if I may ask."

"Speak," Bardoso said, impatient to get on with the raid.

"That large house next to the plaza," the man said, pointing toward a magnificent hacienda. "It belongs to Don Diego Vega, curse him! The beautiful señorita Pulido expects to become his bride tomorrow. If he should perish in this raid, it will cause no sorrow for me."

Bardoso shot back an evil look. "I understand," he said.

"Good," the man said. "As soon as you see the soldiers ride away, you are free to enter the town. *Adios!*" As he spoke the hood of his cloak fell back to reveal his face for the first time.

Bardoso and Sanchez stared at the man's forehead. A ragged scar creased its surface, as red and angry as the day it first had been carved.

"The mark of Zorro," Sanchez gasped.

Before either pirate could speak again, the man vanished into the shadows.

The pirates moved quietly back up the hill to the waiting band of men. "I suspect something of a double deal with that man," Bardoso said. An evil smile crossed his face. "So he wants us to steal a prisoner for him for his share of the loot, does he? Since it leaves all the more for us, I would take a dozen such prisoners."

Sanchez had remained silent, but now he spoke his mind. "How can we trust him when he says the soldiers will be sent away?" he asked.

"I will tell you something," Bardoso said as they joined the impatient band of pirates. "We can trust the soldiers will listen to him. For our friend who bears the Mark of Zorro is Captain Ramon—the *comandante* of the garrison assigned to protect Reina de los Angeles from the likes of us."

TWO

The Raid Begins

Sergeant Pedro Garcia was a giant of a man with a heart as big as his sense of adventure. His fellow soldiers at the garrison at Reina de los Angeles called him Pedro the Boaster because he liked nothing better than to amaze his listeners at the village inn with tall tales.

Sergeant Garcia was an honest soldier who had fought with Zorro months earlier to rid the highway known as El Camino Real of robbers and thieves. When the menace ended, the mysterious Zorro vanished. Though Garcia had no wish for danger to threaten Reina de los Angeles, he secretly longed to be fighting at Zorro's side once again.

As Sergeant Garcia finished telling another of his improbable exploits to his friends from the garrison, a corporal spoke for all of them. "You make it sound as if Señor Zorro sought the safety of your sword instead of the other way around," he said with skepticism.

"Ha!" Sergeant Garcia roared. "The brave heart that beats within this chest needs no protector. If Zorro were here he would tell you—"

"He would tell us the *truth*!" the innkeeper said as he poured more wine for the soldiers. "However, our protector has vanished like smoke, which is lucky for you. Only his brave companions remain. And they are at the great house of Don Diego at this very moment to celebrate his wedding tomorrow to the lovely señorita Lolita Pulido, the fairest maiden in all of California."

Sergeant Garcia raised his glass. "A toast to my friend—our friend—Señor Zorro. May he never have to ride in anger again."

It was true that Garcia had fought on the side of Zorro. But it was just as true he had once fought against him.

Before it was known that Zorro was a defender of justice and not a blackguard highwayman, the garrison had engaged him and his band of caballeros in a dreadful fight. The garrison's commander, Captain Ramon, had fared poorly against Zorro's flashing blade. Zorro had marked the *comandante*'s forehead with the dreaded Z. The revelers at the inn knew in that encounter Sergeant Garcia had stood against Zorro's incredible sword and had come away unscathed. In tribute to his bravery, they let the sergeant's boasts pass.

"Perhaps we could use someone like Zorro now," a new recruit said. "I have heard there are pirates about."

Sergeant Garcia rose from his place at the head of the table. "Mush and nonsense!" he boomed. "No pirate worthy of the name would dare enter Reina de los Angeles as long as they know I am still stationed here." He leaped to the tabletop, drew his sword, and slashed the air clumsily. "Take that for a pirate," he shouted, "and that, and that, and that."

"Well done," the innkeeper laughed, studying the floor. "You have littered my inn with the carcasses of empty rumors. But please, brave sergeant, your boots on my table make a mockery of my inn."

The sergeant clambered from the table, pouting as if he'd been scolded at school. "Mush and non-sense," he mumbled.

Suddenly the inn door flew open. The soldiers snapped to attention. Standing against the moon-light was Captain Ramon. "Sergeant Garcia," he spat. "I could hear your boasts halfway across the plaza." He approached the men. "But if it's pirates you want, then perhaps you shall have your wish. A band of those rogues has been reported by natives to the south. Mount the troop and search the length of El Camino Real until you find them."

The sergeant threw a stiff salute at his com-mander and turned to his companions. "You have heard the captain," he said. "What are you waiting for?"

As the men made for the door Captain Ramon drew Garcia aside. "Leave only one man to guard the garrison," he said quietly. "And prepare my finest horse. I must ride elsewhere to visit a ha-cienda."

Garcia saluted again. "It is done, Señor Coman-dante," he said, and hurried out the door to carry out Captain Ramon's devious orders.

Moments later the trusting sergeant led his troop out of the village as Bardoso and his evil crew watched from the shadowy hills. Reina de los An-geles now lay unprotected.

Not far away at the palatial hacienda of Señor Don Carlos Pulido, the gray-haired caballero watched proudly as his beautiful daughter Lolita prepared for her wedding the next day to Don Diego Vega. His wife, Doña Catalina, stood nearby, quietly ordering servants carrying silks and gowns in and out of the elegant room.

"Tomorrow my daughter becomes the first lady of Reina de los Angeles," the old man said. "As the bride of Don Diego, even the governor would not dare raise his hand against me. My fortunes will grow, and you shall be a great lady."

Señorita Lolita Pulido blushed and smoothed the jet black hair that hung to her shoulders like a mantle of polished ebony. I will marry Don Diego out of love for my father and nothing else, Lolita whispered in her heart of hearts where none could hear. I respect Don Diego, who is a fine and cultured gentleman, she thought, and I could do much worse for a husband, for he does love me. But my own love is with someone else, a caballero of adventure and wild blood who rides a fiery horse and wears a mask of mystery so that even I do not know his real identity. She sighed loudly.

Señor Pulido winked at his wife. "Thoughts of love, is it? But is not your love all the greater when you know Don Diego is also the wealthiest man in town and the son of my great and noble friend, Don Alejandro Vega? This union will create a family of immense riches and great power."

The lovely Lolita's face turned crimson, knowing she concealed a heart-breaking deceit from her father. Though she admired Don Diego, whom she had known since she was a child, she was in love only with Zorro.

Whether Zorro still lived in the land of California or if he had gone elsewhere, nobody knew. Only the band of adventurous caballeros who had ridden at his side still remained in Reina de los Angeles. They had returned to their way of life as young and wealthy sons of the rich landowners, more interested in personal pleasure than hard work. But the caballeros let it be known that if the masked man they knew as Zorro ever needed them again, they would all follow him at the risk of their very lives. All, that is, but one.

Don Diego had not joined their daring band when Zorro led them against the ruthless robbers who plagued El Camino Real. Instead, the soft-spoken Don Diego secretly had left Reina de los Angeles and had not returned until the danger was past, the thieves were jailed, and Zorro himself had vanished without a trace. And though the caballeros still counted Don Diego as one of them, they knew he would not raise a sword in anger, and so would be left behind if Zorro ever returned.

The happy family gathering was suddenly interrupted by a sharp knock on the door. Don Carlos opened it to reveal a messenger dispatched by Don Diego with a note for señorita Lolita.

"I'll read it," the old man said with a sly smile. "There'll be no secrets between them until after they are married." He opened the note. "'I send you my love and await yours in return,'" he read. "Ha! He is a man of few words."

Doña Catalina stepped to her daughter's side and placed a gentle hand on her shoulder. "Perhaps his actions speak more than his words," she said. "I remember our courtship when you took pages and pages to say less than this simple note."

The old man harrumphed loudly and quickly changed the subject. "How goes it in the village?" he asked the messenger who stood ready to take the señorita's reply to Don Diego.

"It is quiet," the man said. "The soldiers have ridden south in search of rumors of pirates. Only the revelry at the house of Don Diego stirs the air. The caballeros sing of their days riding at the side of Zorro."

Señorita Lolita's heart quivered.

"Zorro is no more," Don Carlos said. "His duties as protector and avenger are done. He has vanished."

The messenger shrugged. "Perhaps," he said. "But to hear the caballeros at this very moment, one would wonder if Señor Zorro really has gone."

With a heavy heart Señorita Lolita wrote a brief reply on the back of Don Diego's note and thrust it into the messenger's hand. "Be gone," she said. "Take this to my betrothed and speak no more of Zorro."

The beautiful girl watched the messenger slip out the door into the moonlit night and wished in her heart she could accompany him. Though her true love had vanished, she would be glad to be with his bold companions if only to hear his name spoken from their lips.

Doña Catalina saw the longing that clouded her daughter's delicate face. "Your secret dream will come true soon, my child," Doña Catalina said. "Tomorrow you will be the wife of the man you love."

Señorita Lolita buried her face in her father's broad shoulder. My secret dream can never come true, she thought, fighting back tears. Because tomorrow I will be the bride of Don Diego while the man I love is Zorro!

A merry bunch of richly dressed caballeros gathered around the sumptuous banquet prepared for them by their friend, Don Diego Vega. With jeweled swords dangling from their sides, they did not look the part of men of adventure. But under the leadership of Zorro they had rid El Camino Real of bandits.

"To Zorro," Don Audre Ruiz exclaimed, holding his glass high. Don Audre was Don Diego's best friend. He knew he could speak freely of the mysterious Zorro and not offend their host. Even though Don Diego had not ridden at the side of the elusive "Fox," he showed no embarrassment as the caballeros toasted their missing leader. "To our days riding at his side with blades drawn and the dust of fleeing scoundrels staining our capes," Don Audre continued.

"To the sword of Zorro!" the caballeros shouted. "Wherever it is!"

Don Diego smiled quietly as he watched his friends toast Zorro. Their days as renegade caballeros sworn to protect the innocent were over. To him it seemed only yesterday the governor's men had chased Zorro's band of men up and down El Camino Real, unaware of his real identity.

Those were the days, Don Diego thought. But now I am to be married to the fairest maid in the land and Señor Zorro must be laid to rest. He stood at his place at the head of the heavily laden table. "Enough of this talk of Zorro," he said aloud. "We live in peace thanks to Zorro, but now he is gone. I say lay him to rest and toast instead my bride to be, the fairest maid in the land."

"But what if there is cause?" Don Audre asked.

Don Diego's eyes met those of each man as he glanced around the table. He smiled gently, revealing nothing of his true reasons for trying to turn the talk away from Zorro. "You have all had your say," he said. "Now I shall have mine. The days of adventure are over, my friends. You have fought well and won. The bandits who plagued El Camino Real have been driven away and dare not return. We are rid of the scoundrels for good—"

Don Audre alone dared interrupt his friend. "If you speak of scoundrels, what of Captain Ramon?" he asked. "Why must we endure the likes of him as *comandante* of the garrison?"

The others murmured aloud, but Don Diego quieted them with a gesture of his hand. "It is true, my friend. The captain deserves as much trust as a mountain lion at our backs. But let us not speak of scoundrels. Tonight is a night of joy—"

A loud shout and the heavy slam of the front door shattered the quiet.

"What in the name of the saints is that?" Don Diego asked as a trembling servant dashed into the banquet room.

The poor man was nearly out of his wits with fear. He looked as if he'd seen a ghost, and his hands shook as if palsied. He pointed to the distance beyond the thick walls of the town house. "Men are fighting at the inn, señor," he gasped. "The village is attacked by *pirates*!"

At the edge of Reina de los Angeles, Bardoso called to Sanchez as he watched Sergeant Garcia and the soldiers ride away in search of an empty rumor of pirates. His grim face looked like the devil himself in the moonlight. The town lay unprotected before him.

"They will be gone for hours," Bardoso said to his lieutenant. "Your task will be to capture the señorita Lolita from the hacienda of Don Carlos Pulido. Take six of our fiercest men and go quickly. I don't care what you do to the place, but see to it the girl is unharmed. Now, steal some horses and be off. Once you have her, ride to where we landed. The ship will meet us there before dawn."

"Sí, my chief," Sanchez replied. "But see that I get my share of the loot." Within moments he selected his men and led them north.

Bardoso remained in the shadows for another hour to make certain Sergeant Garcia and his soldiers didn't return unexpectedly. Then he moved toward the open plaza, whispering his deadly orders to the pirates in his trail.

With broadswords drawn and sharp daggers in their belts, the men poured into the unsuspecting town like a horde of rats driven from the sea. Bardoso split them into raiding parties, each with a specific purpose. One group was to steal horses and carts for the ride back to the ship. The others were assigned to raid the large houses of the wealthy, and the shops and stores of the merchants. "Leave the paltry items and take only that which can be easily carried such as jewels and precious metals," Bardoso hissed. Seeing no sentries to shout alarm or soldiers to contest his entry, he ordered that the attack begin.

The foul band of seafaring thieves and cutthroats swarmed over the sleepy town, kicking in doors and smashing through shutters with their terrible blades of steel. They showed no mercy as they tore precious jewels from the throats of terrified women and ripped valuable gold and gems from the hands of men who sought to protect them.

Here and there a brave heart raised a sword against the horde, but the pirates traveled in thick groups while the townspeople scurried alone and unorganized. They were no match for the raiders.

Outnumbered and stunned by the sudden onslaught, the scattered inhabitants were soon overwhelmed. Victory, if such can be said for such a cowardly attack, was soon in the hands of the pirates.

Bardoso was eager to return to the ship. Though he trusted Captain Ramon, the fear that the soldiers might return haunted him. But there was one more grand house to be taken, and he wanted to lead that attack himself.

The pirate chief shouted to his men, who poured into the plaza laden with loot of every precious description.

"Where are the others?" he asked, not wishing to make the final raid with less than a full company of broadswords at his side.

"In the church," a voice replied.

A group of raiders had broken into the large adobe church, which faced the palm-lined plaza. Without regard for the feelings of the believers whose house they now profaned, the pirates clamored toward the altar where they knew the church's treasure would be found.

A balding friar emerged from a room at the side and stopped the men in their tracks. "What do you want here?" he demanded.

"And who are you to ask?" a pirate said, ready to push the frocked man aside.

"I am Friar Felipe," the priest said. "I am in charge here."

"Ho, ho, ho," the pirate roared. "That's a good one. He thinks he's in charge here, fellows. What think you?"

With roars of laughter the pirates pushed past the stunned priest and made for the altar.

"This is sacrilege," Friar Felipe said.

The first pirate spied a gem-studded goblet on the altar. He curled his thick fist around it and lifted the precious golden treasure into the air. "And I say it is loot!" he crowed.

Friar Felipe paled. The goblet was the most valuable item charged to his care. More than its precious metal and rich jewels, it was said the goblet had once been used by a saint, and so was valued beyond any price. To have such men handle it was unthinkable. "You risk your souls to touch it," the friar shouted. "Be gone. Be gone!"

But the pirates, not the type to worry about bald-headed friars or souls already black as the pits of hell, rushed forward.

"I will die first before I let you take it!" the brave priest shouted.

"So be it," the pirate leading the raiding party replied. He brandished his thick broadsword over his head and made for the trembling friar.

"*Stop!*" a booming voice from the rear of the church shouted. It was Bardoso.

"But he has a precious goblet, more valuable than twenty others," the pirate with the raised sword replied. "I claim it for my share of the loot."

A scowl as dark as a sea squall crossed Bardoso's face. Roaring like a bull let loose in a crowd, he leaped forward and in three giant steps faced the surprised pirate. "For this affront, *this* is your share of the loot," he bellowed. And before the startled man could defend himself, Bardoso's broadsword flattened the side of his head and he dropped like a stone.

Bardoso turned to his men as the stunned pirate struggled to his feet. "Neither the friar nor the goblet is to be harmed," he ordered. "Now leave this place."

Meekly, the men obeyed their chief.

Friar Felipe approached Bardoso. "Perhaps you are not as evil as it would seem," he said, a hint of forgiveness in his voice.

"I am as evil as I am," Bardoso replied. "But I do not assault priests and I do not steal from them." Without further explanation, the fierce pirate whirled toward the door and vanished into the darkness.

The friar sat heavily on the stone floor. His hands shook, but relief filled his bones. He turned for a thankful look to the altar where the precious goblet was kept, and his heart leaped in his breast. The sacred treasure was gone!

A bold rush of courage coursed through the friar as he stood and faced the altar. Raising his face toward the dome of the small church he made a vow. "I go," he pledged. "If I do not return with the goblet, I will not return at all!"

THREE

∽

A Masked Mystery Guest

Bardoso had saved the mansion of Don Diego Vega for last. It was the finest house in the town and was sure to be filled with priceless possessions. He grinned evilly as he remembered Captain Ramon's command to pay special heed to Don Diego's house, and to let happen what might to the young caballero, even if it meant a cutlass through the ribs.

Laughing at the commotion of the town behind them, Bardoso led his men to find the house, which stood unguarded.

Inside the elegant house, Don Diego Vega was still entertaining his guests. He sat at the head of a grand table laden with food and drink as his friends talked excitedly among themselves.

Amid the revelry Don Diego became aware of a distant sound that no one else in the room heard. The messenger had said men were fighting at the inn; he had said there was a rumor of pirates in the town. So, as the caballeros revived their stories of fighting at the side of Zorro, Don Diego had listened.

It is the sound of evil deeds, Don Diego thought. He turned to Don Audre Ruiz, his closest friend.

"Please forgive me, Don Audre," he said. "The excitement of the evening has proved too much for me. Will you do the honor of acting as host in my place while I retire to my room? Perhaps if I lie down this giddiness will pass." He rose from his place and slipped quietly away from the table without any of the other caballeros as much as taking notice.

Don Audre watched his friend ascend the stairs. He had a curious look on his face, one which revealed suspicions he dared not entertain openly. The look changed to a sly smile. One day he would speak his secret thoughts to Don Diego. But tonight was not the time.

Once out of sight, Don Diego rushed to his room and hurried across it to the large window that overlooked the town plaza. His keen senses were proved right. Danger was near. A scurvy band of coarse-looking men—pirates—were crossing the plaza headed directly for his house.

"There is something most foul afoot," he said, his voice resolute. He stepped away from the window. "The time has come—as I knew it someday would." Quickly he went to a small paneled section of wall and pushed. The wall opened, and Don Diego slipped inside, then closed the panel behind him.

Bardoso stomped loudly across the square with his dark-hearted men behind him. He left four men at the entrance of Don Diego's house to warn the others if the soldiers returned. Then the pirate chief raised his ugly sword and led his band in attack.

The pirates rushed the huge oak door, and it parted from its thick hinges with a loud roar. The pirate band flooded into the candlelit house, only to stop, stunned by what they found.

Bardoso stared in astonishment at the magnificent room they had entered. It was a huge hall decorated with suits of ancient armor used by the conquistadors. On its walls were polished shields, sharp swords and pikes, and the heads of wild animals, trophies of many successful hunts. Rich tapestries hung from the walls, more elegant than those Bardoso had heard draped the castle of the king of Spain himself. But most astounding of all was the immense table spread with food unlike any he'd ever seen. Giant roasted birds and fatted pigs lay amid brilliant fruits and vegetables prepared for a feast.

And gathered around the table, the true reason for Bardoso's great shock, was a company of twenty handsome young caballeros, dressed to fit the grand occasion.

Bardoso paused in astonishment. The guests, strong and as eager for a contest as young bulls entering a ring, were the gentlemen of Reina de los Angeles. Their grim looks clearly showed they would not take the pirate band's uncouth entry lightly. Bardoso had seen men like these in action before and a quiver of uncommon fear crossed his breast.

There was no time for orders. The caballeros leaped from their chairs around the banquet table, their slim, keen-edged swords quickly drawn.

The pirates, already at arms, raised their thick broadswords over their heads like clubs.

Each man silently chose a foe and the two groups began to close on one another.

"What have we here?" a calm voice said over the clank and shuffle of men preparing for action. All heads turned to the top of the stairs.

It was Zorro. His broad shoulders were draped by the shimmering folds of an elegant black cape. Black pants and a pair of high black boots of burnished leather covered his legs. Bright silver spurs flashed at his heels. His eyes gleamed from within the black silk mask that covered his face. And in his hand, raised high as if in a salute to those gathered around the table, was the gleaming sword of Zorro!

Pirates and caballeros alike held their places. Each band remained silent for their own reasons. The pirates out of shock. The caballeros out of pure joy.

Zorro stood quietly at the head of the stairs and smiled at the pirate chief. "Although you neglected to announce the arrival of yourself and your interestingly clad men, I believe you have erred in entering this house." With his hand grasping his famous jeweled sword he descended the stairs straight toward Bardoso, whose own feet stuck to the floor as if tarred.

"These are my friends," Zorro continued. "They are here by invitation to celebrate a wedding that will take place tomorrow between Don Diego Vega, whose house you dishonor, and Señorita Lolita Pulido. Since I can't imagine you or your quaintly perfumed men numbering among Don Diego's friends, I trust you will leave by the same door you entered."

Bardoso could take no more of Zorro's insults. He kicked over a chair in rage and swirled his huge sword in a circle above his head. "Whoever you are, do you realize you are speaking to Bardoso, king of the pirates?" he roared. "Our black flag and black hearts strike terror on land and on sea—"

Zorro threw back his head and roared with laughter as if he'd been told the moon was made of cheese. He turned to the gallant gentlemen arranged before him, their own swords still drawn, and spoke to Don Audre. "Hear you that, Don

Audre?" he said. "These vermin are here to freeze our hearts with terror."

Don Audre stepped forward, laughing aloud. "What a perfect jest," he said. "Don Diego has arranged a most memorable party and a wonderful joke for us all. It is too bad he is missing it."

Bardoso's face turned as red as the apple stuck in the mouth of the spitted pig on the table before him. "Joke? You dare to call Bardoso a joke?" Enraged, he brought his great sword down, sweeping the end of the table clear of its succulent spread. "This is no joke, you lace-throated fops. Against the wall with you, and the first one who makes a move joins that cooked creature who is doomed to suck an apple while its bones are picked."

Don Audre roared with laughter. "Don Diego has outdone himself, for this joke of his is both a pirate and a poet."

Bardoso could scarcely see through the blood-red rage that thundered through his head. "To the wall," he screeched. "I am the king of this crew."

Zorro stepped forward. "You are the king of the pirates, eh?" he said in a tone that rang of steel. With a move so sudden not a man in the stunned group could see, Zorro leaped to the tabletop. He scattered the banquet feast across the floor with a well-aimed kick and pointed the needlesharp tip of his famous sword at Bardoso's forehead. "You've come here to steal, is that it?"

Bardoso was no longer cowed by the bravery of the mysterious masked man. His sword flashed in the glow of the flickering candles. "And who is to stop me? Surely not you and your toy sword."

"You would insult this good blade?" Zorro demanded. "Not while I live." With that he leaped from the table at Bardoso. The pirate prepared to fend off the whirling point but to his surprise Zorro did not attack. Instead he stepped by the pirate chief and with three flashes of the slim bade he carved three telltale scars into the paneled wall behind Bardoso's head. It was the letter Z.

Bardoso gasped at the sight, recognizing the mark as the same one that Captain Ramon bore on his forehead. "It is the Mark of Zorro!" he exclaimed. "Then *you* are Zorro!"

Zorro faced the pirate chief with narrowed eyes and took one threatening step forward.

"Do not move," Bardoso shouted. "Give us loot or you'll be here in the morning as cold as the stones you'll lie on." It was the last thing in the world the pirate wanted, to fight the young, daring caballeros and their bold leader, but now he had to act or face the loss of his own leadership over his dreaded pirate band.

Zorro turned to his caballeros. "What would you, my friends, hot blood or cold stones?"

The young blades leaped forward. Their swords sliced the air, producing a wail like bitter wind on a stormy sea. But the pirates were ready. The battle was on.

Pirate cutlasses clanged heavily against the caballero's sleek blades, and bright sparks flew each time they met.

Zorro's famous sword scored the air, its dreaded tip flashing like a tiny meteor at the pirate chief who countered with heavy thrusts from his own blade. Zorro's steel made a half dozen passes to Bardoso's one, and to the pirate it seemed he was up against a half score of men. But it was just one on one as the two fought. The room resounded with the thud of boots, the toppling of fine furniture, and the cries of battle.

"So, you are a pirate, are you?" Zorro shouted over the din. He toyed with Bardoso the way a cat does a mouse before making the final leap. "Well, so I might know you ere we meet again, let me leave a sign with you."

With that Zorro lunged forward. With three flicks of his wrist he scored the forehead of the pirate chief with a ragged Z.

"Aaiee!" Bardoso screamed, clutching his forehead as if it had been branded with fire.

"Know it well, Señor Pirate Chief," Zorro said. "For others surely do."

Suddenly the pirates were fighting for their lives. They moved steadily backward toward the door, each fending off the valiant strikes of a caballero.

"To the horses," Bardoso bellowed.

The pirates turned on their heels and raced out of Don Diego's house to where the rest of their crew waited with fine stolen horses. In seconds the dread band was lost in the dust as they kicked their steeds to a gallop and rode out of town.

Zorro and his caballeros ran after them on foot, but it was useless.

"They have stolen our horses," Don Audre said. "They are the best in the land. Even if we found others, we could never outrace our own animals at what they do best."

"But you cannot let them go," a voice cried from the dark. It was Friar Felipe.

"Have they harmed you, too?" Zorro said, clasping the priest's arm.

"It would take more than a pirate's wrath to bring me harm," Friar Felipe said. "But they have stolen the sacred goblet from the church, and that pains me more than death itself."

Zorro stared through the moonlight at the cloud of dust in the far-off hills that marked the path of the fleeing pirates. "I shall do everything in my power to catch them," he said.

"I know you will," the priest said.

The caballeros raised their swords in allegiance to their leader. "We shall see the pirates in chains," they vowed. "Lead and we will follow."

But no sooner had they spoken when a disheveled man staggered out of the shadows. It was the foreman of the great hacienda of Don Carlos Pulido. The man was wounded.

Zorro grabbed the man as he fell to the ground. "What is it?" he asked.

"Pirates," the injured man gasped. "A band of pirates attacked the hacienda of Don Carlos an hour ago while others were attacking the village here."

Zorro suspected the worst. "Yes, yes, go on. What happened?"

"They looted the house," the man said. "They took the horses. They burned the buildings—"

"Yes, yes!" Zorro shouted. "But what of the señorita?"

The man bowed his head. "Do not blame me," he said with a quivering voice. "We fought valiantly. But they have carried away the lovely mistress—"

Zorro's face turned crimson with rage. "Carried her away?"

"To the sea," the foreman said. "They said Señorita Lolita Pulido is to be taken as the prize of some great man."

Zorro clenched his sword so tightly his knuckles whitened. "She has been stolen like a piece of common loot as a prize? *Never!*" he shouted.

"To the rescue," Don Audre called, leaping to the center of the group. "Lead us as you will, Zorro, for by the grace of what's good, we will return her."

Zorro was stunned. His eyes seemed to be fixed on some distant horizon known only to himself. For a moment he appeared to be in a trance. Then the glow of hot blood returned to his cheeks, and the dark power of anger flooded through him.

"Join me now," he shouted, his sword raised high into the air. "We shall ride once again to rid the land of tyrants and thieves. Are you with me?"

To a man the caballeros raised their swords so that the tips met in a bright point that sparkled against the velvet-black night.

Zorro lifted his blade from theirs and, with a move so swift no human eye could follow, he cut the air with three streaks. It was the bold letter Z, his deadly mark.

"We are with you," the caballeros shouted.

"Then to the rescue," Zorro said. "Gather horses from those left behind and follow me to the sea. My faithful Toranado and I will go ahead. We will find a fast ship there we can use to pursue the pirates over the waves. We go!"

As the caballeros hurried to find horses to replace those the pirates had stolen, Zorro went to the secret stable where his black stallion Toranado pawed eagerly at the earth. He quickly saddled the marvelous beast with black leather and silver and soon the two, together again at last, raced like a demon wind through the moonlight toward the distant sea.

FOUR

∞

Zorro Strikes Back

The raid had gone well for the pirates at the fine hacienda of Don Carlos Pulido. Led by the villainous Sanchez, the grim band overwhelmed the servants working in the outbuildings before they could sound the alarm. The way was then clear to the main house where Señorita Lolita and her mother prepared for the next day's wedding to Don Diego.

Sanchez was the first to enter the house. Don Carlos, his hair gray with age, but his back straight and proud as ever, drew his sword. "Pirates!" he shouted.

At the sound of the dread word, Doña Catalina and her beautiful daughter raced to Don Carlos's side, sure his keen sword would protect them. But Sanchez already had his cutlass ready. With a single swipe he toppled the old man, knocking him unconscious.

Sanchez grabbed Señorita Lolita by the arm and dragged her from her father's side. Though Lolita fought valiantly, kicking and tearing at the pirate, she was no match for his brute strength. "Easy with you, wench." Sanchez laughed. "You are not to be harmed for you are to be the prize of a great man."

"Never!" Lolita screamed.

But the girl's screams were in vain. The pirates had the run of the place, sacking it completely. The fine treasures accumulated over a lifetime by Don Carlos were loaded into a cart for the journey to the sea.

Sanchez stole the finest horse from Don Carlos's stable and placed Lolita in the saddle in front of him. "To the ship," he ordered.

The pirates rode off, leaving a sobbing Doña Catalina to tend to her wounded husband. The gallant old gentleman struggled to his feet, and called to his foreman. "Find a horse," he commanded. "Ride to town and tell Don Diego of this foul deed. If you love the señorita, spare not the horse or yourself until your task is done. Now go!"

Señorita Lolita had fainted when Sanchez threw her into the saddle. Now she came to as the pirate band, following an old trail used by traders, rode at full gallop toward the sea.

Sanchez's horse stumbled over the coarse trail and Señorita Lolita, terrified for her life, hung on. She did not know where the pirates were taking her or whose prize she was to be. She shuddered at what lay ahead.

Then her fear lifted as she remembered who she was. She was a Pulido, a member of a proud, brave family who had wrested a fabulous fortune from the dry hills. Whatever her fate, her proud blood would not let her down. She would remain a Pulido to the very end.

After many hours the exhausted horses reached the sea. The pirates unloaded the loot and corralled the spent animals. The tiny señorita was bound by the wrists and forced to sit on the cold ground, still a helpless prisoner.

Sanchez ordered a giant bonfire built to signal the ship, and the roaring flames sent a cascade of sparks into the night sky. Soon Bardoso arrived, leading his raiders and a fortune in loot.

"How fared you, Sanchez?" Bardoso asked, searching the darkness for signs of more treasure.

"We have the girl," Sanchez replied.

Bardoso considered Lolita as if examining a prize animal. "No wonder our benefactor wished her stolen," he said. "She is fitting pretty for a king."

Lolita turned away, not giving the pirate chief so much as a glance.

Bardoso whispered to Sanchez, "We have what we went for, but there is more to tell. Our raid interrupted a band of lace-throated caballeros who see themselves as fit to cross swords with us. If they are so bold to pursue us, we must be ready. Place a sentinel atop that high peak to warn us if anyone wishes to contest our victory."

"It is done, my chief," Sanchez said, and directed a man to climb the peak overlooking the place where the band awaited their ship. The guard's dark silhouette paced back and forth, watching the rear approaches.

The pirates piled their ill-gotten haul near the shore to be ready to load on the small boats that would take them to the ship. Among the stolen goods were bottles of fine wine and the pirates drank as they worked. Soon they were laughing and singing, praising their chief and their own bravery.

Lolita watched the sentinel high above the beach as he paced back and forth. Suddenly another figure appeared beside him and the two began to struggle. Oh, if only it could be someone to save me, she thought.

Bardoso also saw the struggle on the clifftop. "To the cliff," he shouted to his drunken men. "Someone has discovered us."

A half-dozen armed pirates began to clamber up the steep slope, but before they were halfway up a scream pierced the air, followed by a dull thud from the sandy beach behind them.

Bardoso turned and stared at the sentinel lying on the sand at his feet. He lifted a glowing brand from the fire and brought it near the fallen man's face. "By the saints," he swore, his eyes bulging in disbelief. On the man's cheek was a freshly carved Z.

"Look," said Sanchez. "What's that under his belt?"

Bardoso gingerly plucked off the scrap of paper that had been fastened there. The note was written in crimson, as if by the point of a sword.

"'Señors,'" Bardoso read aloud. "'Your treachery will be punished. Z.'"

For a moment the night was silent. Only the gentle lapping of the waves could be heard. Then Bardoso shook his thick fist at the peak above them. "It is the accursed Zorro, the land pirate who perceives himself a fox. After him!"

A band of pirates led by Sanchez began to scale the cliff. As they climbed Sanchez wondered why his chief did not join them. He had not yet seen the scar on Bardoso's face, nor did he know that when Bardoso matched swords with Zorro at the banquet, the caballero could have had him at any moment. Sanchez could not even guess at the fear the pirate captain had for the daring Zorro.

The pirates reached the summit only to find there was no trace of the man who had killed their comrade.

As they hastened back to the beach where boats from their ship were already being loaded with loot, Sanchez paused but did not dare turn to face the sound that came from behind him in the darkness. It was a chilling, mocking laugh.

The boats were quickly loaded, and Señorita Lolita was placed in the bow of the lead boat, her wrists still bound. Bardoso sat near her, intrigued by her beauty and puzzled by her haughty, unyielding stares.

"It seems you have a protector," Bardoso said, referring to the man who had appeared atop the cliff.

Lolita faced her tormentor boldly. Thinking that perhaps it had been Don Diego, she said bravely, "If I do, Señor Pirate, it is time for you to feel afraid."

"Do you think I fear this fellow?" Bardoso laughed.

"He is no ordinary fellow," she answered. "He is a caballero with the finest, bravest blood flowing in his veins and is ten times the match for the likes of you any day."

Bardoso's blood boiled. He had already felt the sting of Zorro's sword and knew the truth of what the girl said even if she was speaking of Don Diego while it was Zorro whom the pirate had encountered. "By my naked blade," he roared, "if you were mine and not the prize of a great man, I would cast you into the sea for speaking thus. Ha! But what care I. You'll forget your precious protector soon enough, when you are in the arms of the man I deliver you to."

"Never!" Señorita Lolita said coldly. "As for you, do not speak to me again. Your words are like stable litter and foul the air."

Rage burned the pirate chief's cheeks. He turned away from her, unable or unwilling to face her continued scorn. "See that she does not throw herself into the sea," he ordered. Then he busied himself with the loot that was piled heavy in the boat.

The young girl lay her head down on the rough gunwale so none of the men could see the tears that welled in her eyes. Her hair hung over the side like delicate lace, and her hands trailed in the water that splashed at the bow as the heavy boat made for the black ship anchored a mile offshore.

The other boats followed. Soon they would all be aboard the pirate craft and hope for rescue, if there ever had been any, would fade to nothing.

Zorro stood on the cliff overlooking the sea. His face was creased with anger as he watched the line of boats rowing steadily toward the tall-masted pirate ship. If he did not act now, he would not get another chance.

He strode to the end of the cliff where a point reached out over the sea below. He picked out a tiny spot between two jagged rocks on the surging ocean below, secured his sword at his belt, and without a further glance, dived headlong off the cliff. The hissing sea rose to meet him.

He had judged the waves' rise and fall with perfection. He struck the water when it was deepest. A split second too soon or too late and he would have plunged to the bottom and broken his neck. He struggled to the surface. Wasting no time, he fixed his bearings and struck out for the lead boat, swimming strongly but silently like a man possessed. With the strength and grace of a sea creature, Zorro swam unseen alongside the boat.

Sitting in the bow was the lovely señorita. Zorro fought the urge to call out to her. Had it been daylight every eye would have seen him, but darkness shielded him and allowed him to pursue his bold venture.

Each forward surge of the boat stung Lolita's beating heart for it put rescue farther behind. She tried to maintain her courage, but alone and frightened, on an unfamiliar sea, her bravery was fast fading.

The young girl was as confused as she was frightened. Time and again the pirate chief had said she was to be the prize of a great man. But she wondered what manner of greatness would possess such a man to order her kidnapped. She did not want to think about her fate, but each time the wind brought the stench of the unwashed pirates past her, fear once again filled her mind.

Lolita closed her eyes tightly and dreamed of rescue. Her hands, still bound, trailed over the boat's rough side, splashed by the waves.

And then something touched her hands. It was not the touch of the playful water but the firm, tender touch of something alive. And then again, the same touch. And she knew it was the touch of a hand. A thrill ran through her as she felt the gentle caress of warm lips against the back of her tightly bound hands.

Lolita's cheeks flamed scarlet. Her heart came within a breath of standing still. Just beneath the sparkling surface of the ocean was a face, and smiling up through the water with a fire in his eyes that spoke more than a chorus of words was Zorro!

The young girl nearly swooned. Her mind raced to somehow understand how this could be. Yet it was true. Zorro was with her, swimming boldly alongside her captor's boat with no thought for himself, ready to rescue her at the first opportunity.

Lolita wanted to speak out but dared not. She held Zorro's gaze with her own. Her eyes watched his lips as they formed the words, "Courage. I'll be near."

Then Zorro's face sank from sight. Lolita was more alone than she had ever been in her life. But she had no more time to think. The boat thudded noisily against the side of the pirate ship and coarse hands quickly lifted her aboard.

Bardoso shouted commands and the men made ready for sea. The loot was loaded aboard. The unwilling captive was placed under guard. The pirates had no thought except to be clear of this place and on their way.

Amid the flurry of orders and commands that sent the men scurrying madly around the decks, no one saw the dark-caped figure clamber from the sea up the moss covered anchor chain moments before it was raised and the ship turned to sea.

Zorro was aboard the pirate craft with vengeance in his heart and his gleaming sword at his side.

FIVE

A Caballero's Near

Bardoso led Señorita Lolita to a tiny, grimy cabin below decks. A rat scurried out the door as he bid her enter. "It's not a palace," he said. "But with this torch to keep away the four-legged rats and a strong door to keep out those with two legs, you'll be safe until I turn you over to the man who will claim you."

Lolita said nothing. She simply ignored the pirate chief.

"Too good to speak to a pirate, are you?" Bardoso said with a scowl. "Well, you may change your mind when you meet the man who had me steal you." He put his hand on the door. "Is there anything you want or need?"

Lolita's face flushed with anger. "Yes," she spat. "I want you to leave."

Bardoso fumed. "Ha!" he snorted. "Deliver me from the likes of proud women like you."

He fastened the torch to the wall and slammed the door behind him. The loud clank of a heavy bolt shot home secured the door from the outside.

Lolita tried to stop her hands from trembling as she realized that she was imprisoned on a pirate ship. For the first time her heart filled with despair.

The señorita sat on a crude bunk nailed to the wall and studied her dim prison. The ship was old

43

and full of cracks. A single porthole, much too small to crawl through, showed the silver disk of the moon in the night sky outside. Her cabin prison was a mere eight feet wide and just as narrow. She glanced at the rear wall. An odor from it suggested it was used to store supplies that had seen fresher days. The wall was creased with wide cracks, but the boards themselves were far too thick to break down.

Lolita sighed. Her thoughts raced back through the terrible events of the night that had begun with such happiness. She thought of her poor father lying wounded on the ground and of her mother, bent over him. And she thought of Zorro. She sensed in her heart he was nowhere near, but was left behind to drown.

Suddenly a hissing sound startled her. The keen point of a sword was sticking from a crack in the storeroom wall, wagging up and down as if signaling.

She followed the sword point with fascination, not knowing what to think. As the point traced a letter in the dank air Lolita covered her mouth lest her cry of joy be overheard. It was the letter Z.

"Zorro?" Lolita whispered, half-afraid her hopes would be crushed.

"Sí, señorita," a muffled voice from the storeroom replied. "It is Zorro, at your service."

"The saints be thanked." Señorita Lolita sighed. Then her eyes darkened. "But you are alone. What can you hope to do against a band of rogues such as those who guide this foul ship?"

"Have you so little faith in my ability to protect you?" Zorro's voice was teasing.

"Oh, no, it's not that," Lolita said. "But there is such danger."

Zorro laughed aloud. "Danger? Here is what I think of danger. I will sing for your captors so they will know how little I think of their black hearts."

"No," Lolita pleaded. "They will hear you."

"That's exactly what I want," Zorro replied. "They will hear my voice and be struck by terror to know that I am here."

"You are brave," Lolita whispered. "But there are eighty of them and only one of you. You must not tempt a fate that will see us both dead."

"Do not speak of death, my little one," Zorro answered. "So long as I draw a breath, you must know that I will stand by to protect the helpless.

"I will be going now," Zorro said through the tiny crack. "But I will see your lovely face through the porthole before the dawn comes."

"You would risk capture just to see me?" Lolita asked.

"I would risk my very life," the masked caballero answered.

Lolita listened. Muffled footsteps followed by silence told her Zorro had left the storeroom. Just as her heart started to grow heavy again with loneliness she heard a voice raised in song. It was Zorro, singing a taunting song to the pirates as he said he would. She listened to the words.

"*Atención*! A caballero's near!
To guard the one to his heart most dear!
To love, to fight, to jest, to drink!
To live the life and never shrink!
His blade is bright, his honor, too!
Atención! A caballero's near!"

Lolita put her head against the harsh wooden partition. Zorro's voice lifted her spirits. She remembered times when the caballeros serenaded her at her father's hacienda and Don Diego spoke his love for her in a similar song. "Oh, Zorro," she said aloud. "Must you be so bold and brave to risk everything?"

There was no reply from the other side of the wall, only the voice of Bardoso roaring at his men. "Who dares sing such a song?"

"It's a ghost song," Sanchez said aloud, and one of the men heard him. A superstitious lot, the words passed from one pirate to another. "A ghost song," they repeated, shuddering with fear.

"By my blade, there'll be ghosts aplenty if more of this nonsense meets my ears," Bardoso shouted, whipping his cutlass from his belt. "Get to work and forget this talk of ghosts, for there are none aboard my ship."

But as he spoke the song sounded again. "Atención! A caballero's near—"

"It is a ghost song," Sanchez said.

Bardoso's flat blade passed within a hair's breadth of his lieutenant's nose. "No more talk of ghosts," he ordered. "It's a trick by some scurvy knave among you who won't fare as well when I find him. Now get back to work."

The men silently returned to their work, but each listened for the return of the ghostly song.

A pirate slinked through the shadows, moving toward Bardoso who stood at the helm of his ship. "Chief?" the man whispered.

Bardoso turned. "Why aren't you working with the rest?" he growled.

The man had something beneath his ragged shirt. "I have something for you," he said. "A bit of loot far too fine to store with the rest."

"Loot?" Bardoso said, his greedy eyes turned toward the man.

"Yes, my chief," the sniveling pirate whispered. "I took it myself from the church in Reina de los Angeles."

Bardoso's eyes narrowed and a cloud of doubt passed behind them. "The church?" he said with a quiver in his voice.

The pirate unfolded his shirt, and held up the gleaming golden goblet encrusted with fine gems. "Yes. This precious goblet. I took it from the friar during the raid." He handed the priceless booty to Bardoso.

Bardoso leaped back as if the thing were a venomous snake coiled to strike. "Away with it!" he cried. "I do not want to touch it or see it. It is a thing under the protection of the friar. Here, it brings ill omens."

"But, chief—" the pirate thief pleaded.

"Away with it," Bardoso yelled. "Ill luck will follow the man who possesses it. Get rid of it or keep it yourself. I do not want it. I knew a man who once robbed a church, and I do not want to remember what happened to him."

"I may keep it?" the astounded man asked.

"I will not touch it," Bardoso said. "And I call upon the saints to witness that I have not. Now be gone with it."

Zorro smiled mischievously as he finished his taunting song. He knew it would set the pirates' nerves on edge. When he was sure the way was clear he opened the storeroom door and peered into the narrow passage outside. The heavy thud of boots on deck and the whistle of wind through the rigging were the only sounds that greeted him.

The bold caballero sneaked to a ramshackle ladder at the end of the passage and quietly climbed to the deck. He was familiar with the ship because he had seen her type before.

With his sword muffled by his hand, Zorro crawled along the rail, safely hidden from the glare of torches. He paused to study the situation.

Amidships the pirates still labored with the loot under the hot curses of Bardoso. A fresh wind drove the ship at a good speed through the water, and the rigging fairly hummed. As the ship rolled, Zorro reached out a hand to steady himself. His hand came to rest on a tub of small metal bolts used to mend brass, and he grinned as an idea came to him.

In the distance, behind Bardoso and his men was the ship's huge bell. Zorro stood, braced himself, and took careful aim at the bell. Then he let fly one of the bolts. It flew straight to its mark, and the bell rang as loudly as if hit by a musketball.

The pirates jumped at the sudden sound, their eyes widening with fear.

Bardoso grabbed his sword handle. "Which of you fools did that?" he bellowed.

Sanchez stared at the bell. "No man was near it," he said. "Even though I heard it myself."

Bardoso looked up into the rigging. "Perhaps something fell from a spar," he said.

No sooner had he spoken when the bell rung out again, this time even louder than before. The pirates rushed together in a circle, their swords drawn.

"It's a ghost bell!" one of them shrieked, and instantly the others took up his cry.

"There is no ghost," Bardoso shouted above the din. "Now get back to work." He strode boldly toward the bell to prove there was nothing to fear, but inside he was uneasy. He called for the man who had stolen the goblet from Friar Felipe.

"Did you keep the goblet?" Bardoso asked the man.

The man nodded. "Yes, chief," he said. "Do you want it now?"

Bardoso backed away from the man as if he had the plague. "By the hounds of hell, no! Keep it away from me. And if misfortune comes to any man or to this ship because of that goblet, you'll pay for your deed on the ocean floor—"

Before Bardoso finished speaking the bell rang out again, its crisp sound rolling over the ship like mysterious thunder.

The man with the goblet ran into the darkness, and Bardoso, his face white with fear, approached the bell so close he could reach out and touch it.

"The man who is playing this tiresome trick will be shark-bait when I learn his name," the pirate chief screamed. He stood his ground near the bell knowing he had to show courage or lose face. He ordered two men to stand by the bell with blazing torches. The men obeyed even though the fear of ghosts had them trembling in their boots.

The bell remained silent. Zorro grinned. He had accomplished his purpose—to make the crew nervous. Then, as bold as ever, he tied one end of a stout line around the ship's rail and made a loop in the other. Testing it first to see if it would hold his weight, he slipped one leg into the loop and swung over the side of the ship. He lowered himself slowly toward the dim light which glowed from a lone porthole deep down the huge craft's side. When he reached it, he peered inside.

"Zorro!" Señorita Lolita gasped as she stared into the face of her protector. "You are risking all—"

"And I would do it again for just one look at you," Zorro said, still grinning at his own bold deed. "Danger is the spice of life, señorita."

"Oh, Zorro!" Lolita said. "Above you are dangerous men who hate you and below you is the sea that would snatch you into its mouth as a leopard eats a mouse."

"But I am Zorro," the bold adventurer laughed.

"But what of me if you are a dead Zorro?" Lolita replied. "Go back to your hiding if you truly care for me."

The smile vanished from Zorro's lips. "It's true," he said. "This is a great risk, but I had to see you for you are the most beautiful señorita in all the world."

Lolita reached out her hand to Zorro's and they touched.

"I will go now that you have given me the strength I need to undo the villains who have done this to you."

"Go, Zorro," Lolita said softly. "And may the saints protect you."

Zorro swung away from the porthole. "Adios, my señorita. Adios!"

Their eyes met for an instant longer, and then the bold adventurer was gone.

As Lolita curled up on her lonely bunk, afraid of what might befall her brave protector, Zorro climbed back to the deck. He hid the rope and then secreted himself where he could watch the pirates without being seen.

Most of the loot was stored away. No sailors were in the high rigging. Bardoso was cursing a group of men near the opposite rail as Sanchez listened. Zorro's anger flared when he realized that the man Sanchez was second in command and that it was he who had abducted the beautiful Lolita.

When Sanchez left the group and ambled across the deck to where Zorro hid, Zorro saw an opportunity to increase fear among the superstitious pirates. He drew his famous sword and tested its deadly tip in the chill night air.

As Sanchez passed in front of a flaming torch, which momentarily blinded him, Zorro struck. With a quick flick of the famous steel blade he laid his dread mark on Sanchez's bare forehead.

Sanchez let out a fearsome shriek as his brow burned with sudden pain. Zorro slipped deeper into the darkness.

Bardoso yelled from across the deck. "Is that you, Sanchez? Wailing like a woman?"

Sanchez staggered toward Bardoso, still clutching his head.

"By the dogs of darkness," Bardoso swore. "It is the mark of the accursed Zorro!"

Sanchez's eyes were wide with fear. "It was a demon. There was no man," he said. "It was a ghost."

"There are no ghosts aboard this ship," Bardoso bellowed. "It was a man of flesh and blood."

Sanchez stared at his chief defiantly. "And I say I saw no man and saw no blade though my eyes were open wide. I say 'twas a ghost."

Just then, as if to make the point all the better, the big brass bell near the pirates' heads boomed again. Zorro had hurled another bolt to add to the fun.

Bardoso drew his heavy cutlass and brandished it as the crew shrieked in terror. Secretly the pirate chief wished for dawn; the events of the night were getting on his nerves.

"The ghost," Sanchez said, staring at the bell, which had just pealed though no human hand was near it.

"Any more talk of ghosts and you'll *all* be ghosts,"
Bardoso shouted. "I say it is Señor Zorro himself
who is aboard, or one of you who is playing his
part."

Sanchez continued to shudder. "I say it is a
ghost."

Bardoso placed the point of his cutlass at the tip
of Sanchez's nose. "The men are superstitious fools,
Sanchez," he said. "But you are supposed to have
some sense, else I would not have you second in
command. Now, no more talk of ghosts. And when
we find this Zorro fellow, he will despise the day he
toyed with Bardoso."

Zorro chuckled softly from his hiding place. Even
though his mission was of great seriousness, he was
having grand fun and he could not resist a parting
shot before returning to his hiding place. He clambered up the rigging and let fly a volley of bolts,
aiming them one by one at the startled men below.

The men screamed aloud as the bolts struck
them. "I've been hit by the devil," a pirate shouted.

"The ghost has touched me," another screamed.

Bardoso raced in circles trying to control his
men, but their fear overwhelmed his dark threats.

Finished with his game, Zorro slipped down the
rigging, and hurried to the safety of the unused
storage room next to Lolita's barred prison. He
made at once for the crack that opened into her
dank cell. "Señorita!" he whispered.

The little señorita sat up with a start. "Zorro!" she
exclaimed. "I feared for your life."

Zorro laughed. "Do not worry. I have toyed with
these 'bold' men, but I would not toy with your life."

Footsteps in the passage outside the two adjoining rooms halted all conversation. A pirate opened

the door to the señorita's cell. "I have brought you food at the chief's command," the pirate said.

Lolita turned away with disgust. "And does your chief think I would eat it?"

"I am ordered· to give you food," the pirate said, and placed the plate near the señorita's bunk.

Lolita stared at the man. "I accept nothing from your chief or from you." As she spoke she looked at the food, and the label on a small bottle of wine filled her with painful memories. The wine was from her father's estate, bottled by his own hand. "Leave me alone," she said.

The pirate moved closer. "You may eat the food or throw it out the porthole," he said. "But perhaps you have a kiss for me before I go."

Lolita's anger flared. "Your chief will hear of this outrage," she cried. "Now get out!"

The man persisted, moving toward her, his greedy eyes fixed on her delicate lips. "A single kiss," he said.

"I would rather die!" Lolita exclaimed.

"Am I such an ugly one to deserve talk like that?" the pirate said angrily. He grabbed for her arm and pulled her toward him.

Lolita fought the man's coarse advances, but she was no match for his brute strength.

As he pinned her against the wall there was a sudden hiss from the crack in the wall. The slim, deadly tip of Zorro's sword flickered into the room, struck, and was as quickly withdrawn. The pirate screamed in pain and leaped back. A red blaze was scratched deep into his bare arm. He stared at it for a moment and then turned for the door.

But Bardoso blocked his way.

Zorro's sword had saved the señorita, but now she was in even greater danger.

Lolita braced herself.

Bardoso barged into the tiny room and saw in an instant what had happened. Or so he thought. He looked at the pirate with a scowl. "You cur," he said. "You'll be punished for this." Then he turned to Lolita. "What a bold one you are to protect your virtue with nothing more than your fingernails and a woman's righteous scorn. I have half a mind to keep you for myself."

Lolita shuddered. But Bardoso made no move. Instead he took a small dagger from his belt and handed it to the girl. "You may keep the dagger," he said. "If anyone else dares to disobey my commands that you are to be untouched, you will know what to do."

Bardoso faced Lolita as he prepared to lock the door again. "I will deliver you to the man who has helped arrange these things," he said. "But if for some reason that fails, I will claim you for myself." He slammed the heavy door, and the iron bolt fell into place.

Zorro had watched the whole thing through the narrow crack, helpless to do anything. "Señorita!" he whispered when the pirate chief was gone.

But Lolita did not hear. Exhausted by the terrors of an extraordinary day, she fell into a deep slumber on her tiny cot to await what dawn might bring.

The sun didn't rise in the moldy storeroom Zorro used as a hiding place. Instead the room turned from black to gray as a small ray of sun finally penetrated the gloom. The brave caballero put his lips to the crack in the wall and called, "Señorita!" But the brave maiden was lost in deep sleep.

Zorro thought about his situation. He was a man of action and it was action he craved. He was certain his good friend Don Audre Ruiz and the bold caballeros had located a trading schooner and were on the pirate ship's trail at this very moment. But what will happen when they catch up? he wondered. We are greatly outnumbered by these fierce pirates. He smiled, secretly looking forward to the meeting.

A noise from the adjoining room caught Zorro's attention. He peered through the slender crack. Sanchez had entered the senorita's cell and was calling her awake.

"Señorita," the pirate said, "the chief commands you to appear on deck."

Lolita opened her eyes. There was no fear in them even though the strange surroundings gave her a moment's hesitation. She remembered where she was and what had happened.

"I am a Pulido," Lolita answered. "I obey no commands of brutes." She got a good look at Sanchez, whom she recognized immediately. "And you," she said. "You are the beast who struck my father down and stole me from my home and family."

Sanchez, feeling the heat of her anger, did not dare venture closer. "Say what you will," he said, "but you must do as my chief commands. Come with me to the deck."

"I go," Lolita said defiantly, "but of my own choice and not at a dog's command."

Zorro watched through the tiny crack as the two disappeared from the room. Suddenly he feared for Lolita. He did not believe for a moment that Bardoso only wanted to talk to her. "I must follow them," he said.

Zorro let himself out of the storeroom and scrambled up the rickety stairway to the deck. Luckily, there were no pirates about. He hurried to a place where he could watch without being seen and crouched there to wait.

A moment later Sanchez and Señorita Lolita appeared on deck. A few of the crew who were not sleeping or idly watching flying fish dart in and out of the water stared as the beautiful captive walked forward to where Bardoso waited.

"Strange things happened on my ship during the night," Bardoso said. "Perhaps you know something of the truth about them."

"If I did, I would not tell them to the likes of you," Lolita replied.

Bardoso clenched his broadsword. "By my naked blade, I do not have to take such insolence from a prisoner aboard my ship. I demand you tell me what you know."

Lolita ignored the pirate, turning her head toward the open sea.

Frustrated, Bardoso put his lips close to her ear. "Tell me, you with the biting tongue," he said. "Is it possible this Señor Zorro is aboard?"

Lolita did not flinch. Bardoso, his anger building to purple rage, clenched his fists together as if he could squeeze an answer from the haughty maiden's silent throat. "Is this Zorro fellow aboard?" he roared.

Lolita smiled at her captor. "Have you seen him?" she asked demurely. Then, noticing that both Bardoso and Sanchez bore the fresh mark of her beloved, she taunted the pirate chief further. "I do see you and your lieutenant bear his mark."

Bardoso threw his arms up and shouted to the topmast in a fit of rage. "Let me get my hands on him and you'll see what price he'll pay for his insolence," he bellowed. "You'll watch your protector die."

Caught unawares by the threat, Lolita clasped her throat as she uttered a cry of fear. Bardoso whirled. He saw the truth of her gesture.

"So he is aboard, eh?" he cried triumphantly.

"I have not said so," Lolita replied.

"But you will," Bardoso spat. "You fail to realize you are my prisoner, and I can do with you what I will. If you should 'accidentally' fall into the sea to be food for the sharks, I can tell the man whose prize you are to be whatever story I choose and he will believe me."

Lolita shuddered, knowing that Bardoso spoke the truth.

"Now tell me, señorita of the hot blood," Bardoso said in a softer tone. "What do you know of this Zorro? Did you scratch my man in your cabin last night. Or was it your protector's sword?" He grabbed Lolita's arm and squeezed it tightly in his giant fist. "Tell me!"

Zorro watched helplessly. His hand was on his sword, ready to leap to the rescue of his beloved when suddenly a voice from forward froze him in his tracks.

"Sail ho!" the forward lookout shouted. "A sail! A sail!"

The pirate crew raced to the rail. Over the horizon and bearing down fast on the pirate ship was another ship, its white sails gleaming in the morning sun.

Hope beat in Zorro's breast. It was a trading schooner. If only it bears my comrades, the bold caballero wished silently.

Bardoso screamed orders to his men, and the pirate ship turned farther out to sea to prepare for battle.

Zorro eagerly studied the approaching ship. If he knew for certain it carried his friends, he was confident he could begin a fight with the pirates on his own and hold them until help arrived.

The second ship followed the pirate vessel's every move. If it were just a trading schooner, it would have kept its course along the coast. Zorro grew confident help was on its way.

"It hoists another sail," a pirate shouted. All hands turned to watch.

Zorro, too, saw the fresh sail unfurl, and his fears vanished. Splashed across the full width of the broad sheet of white canvas was the letter Z in bright red paint.

Bardoso saw the bold Z emblazoned on the pursuing ship's sail and realized the danger that was fast approaching. With Lolita's frail arm still clenched in his grip, he began to shake the brave young girl. "Speak," Bardoso shouted. "If that is your rescue, and if Señor Zorro is aboard my ship, your fate is sealed. Now tell me, where is Zorro?"

Lolita glared into Bardoso's eyes with a steely stare. "For me this conversation has ended," she said.

Zorro saw Bardoso's grip tighten. His heart ached for his beloved as she cried out in pain at Bardoso's rough handling. He could take it no more. He tore his short dagger from his belt and hurled it deftly through the air on a course aimed straight for the pirate chief's arm. But Bardoso moved at the last moment, and the dagger stuck into the mast behind him, quivering loudly.

One of the pirates had seen Zorro as he stepped briefly into view to hurl the steel shaft. "There!" he shouted. "A man who is not one of us."

Bardoso dropped Lolita who fell to the deck. His eyes were fixed on Zorro, who now faced the full pirate band alone. "It is Zorro!" he bellowed. "Take him! An extra share of loot to the man who does."

Their lust for stolen riches drove the pirates to a frenzy. They raced across the deck toward Zorro whose back was to the rail.

Zorro glanced at the heavy rigging, draped like spider webbing from the tall masts overhead. He leaped for a rope ladder and lifted himself hand over hand above the cries and shouts of the armed men.

The brave caballero darted through the maze of ropes like a monkey. Climbing up one thick spar and sliding down another, he was a moving target for the pirates whose futile attempts to stop him with their swords only spurred Zorro to more and more daring. Each time he swooped to the deck his sword caught a surprised pirate who fell to the deck before another could take his place.

One by one Zorro felled the fierce pirates with his famous sword. He dropped to the deck and quickly dispatched three men to the sea at once. Then he leaped back to the ropes and scurried to another section of the ship to fight still more.

"Seize him, you dogs," Bardoso screamed. But Zorro was more than a match for the pirate blades. He whirled overhead like a spinning top, the bitter point of his sword striking again and again.

For a moment he was cornered. Three broad-backed men with scarred bodies and dark steel blades backed him against the rail. Zorro's sword whistled a deadly tune as it cut through the air, disarming one, then another, and finally the third man. "You're no match for a caballero," Zorro shouted as he raced into the rigging again.

Bardoso watched in disgust as his men were out-witted by the daring man in black who used the pirate ship as if it were his own.

Lolita watched in horror as a group of pirates attacked Zorro with the determination of mad dogs. "Beware!" she shouted.

Zorro saw the attack coming, and lifted himself over the pirates' heads to land behind them, a step away from Lolita. He bowed like a gentleman and kissed her softly on the hand, defying the pirates behind him with the flat of his back, then he was in the air again before they could regroup.

But the pirates had fate on their side. As Zorro clambered up a spar his boot struck a slippery spot, and his grip failed. He plunged to the deck, his outstretched hands grasping empty air.

Lolita screamed as Zorro plummeted to the deck and landed with a crushing blow that rendered him unconscious.

"Bind him!" Bardoso shouted as his men surrounded the fallen caballero.

Tight lashings were spun around the helpless Zorro's wrists and a heavy weight tied to them. A pirate dashed his face with cold sea water, and the caballero awakened to the sinister stares of twenty armed men.

"So, you are mine at last," Bardoso said with a grin. "Now I can repay you for this mark you placed on my forehead, señor."

Bardoso gave a signal and the pirates forced Zorro to his feet. "To the rail with him," Bardoso shouted. "And hold the girl. I want her to see what comes from treachery like his."

The pirates pushed Zorro toward a long, narrow plank that was placed so its far end hung over the dark water below.

Zorro knew what his fate was to be.

"No!" Lolita screamed. "You must not do this thing."

Bardoso roared with laughter. "What sweet revenge," he said. Then he turned to Zorro. "Now, Señor Zorro, prepare to descend to a watery grave." He motioned to a pirate to place Zorro's sword in the caballero's belt. "You may need your famous sword to fight demons."

"Give me a chance to fight for my freedom," Zorro said. "I will take on two, three, as many of your men as you say—"

"And chance losing you to your friends, whose ship dogs us like a swarm of bees seeking honey?" Bardoso said. "Never. However, as a sign of my generosity, you may say good-bye to the señorita. Captain Ramon will claim her soon and—"

Zorro shot a burning glance at Bardoso who realized he had let slip the name he'd kept secret until now. "So, it is Ramon," he said.

"So what?" Bardoso said with a scowl. "The knowledge will do you little good now. To the sea with him."

Ten armed pirates with drawn swords forced Zorro to the end of the plank. He hung suspended for a moment over the rushing waves, his hands tightly bound. Don Audre's ship was in the distance, too far away to help. And Zorro's beloved Lolita, horrified as she watched the dread scene unfold, was as unable to help him. The brave caballero's fate was sealed.

"Give him to the sea!" Bardoso shouted.

"Zorro!" Lolita screamed.

The plank was tipped. With Lolita's cry ringing in his ears, Zorro dropped to the sea as if he were made of lead. In an instant he was gone.

SIX

To the Rescue

Zorro's trusted friend Don Audre Ruiz had taken immediate charge of the caballeros the moment Zorro rode off in hot pursuit of the pirates. The treacherous Captain Ramon had not returned, and Sergeant Garcia was still far to the south. If the pirates were to be caught, it would be up to the caballeros.

"We need horses," Don Audre shouted.

"The good mounts are all gone," a caballero said. "Only these sorry creatures remain."

"Then we must use them," Don Audre said. "There is no time to waste."

Without changing from their elegant silks and satins or exchanging their splendidly jeweled swords for clothing and weapons more fitting a battle with pirates, the caballeros rode off.

"The pirate band has too much of a lead on us," Don Audre said as he directed his band of angry men toward the coast. "They'll be out to sea before we reach the shore. Our only hope to overtake them is to find a trading schooner."

Driving their poor mounts as fast as they dared, the caballeros soon reached a hill overlooking the shore. A man whom Don Audre recognized emerged from the shadows. "Caballeros," he called to the dusty riders. "I saw the pirates take to their ship. They had a girl with them and much loot."

Don Audre jumped from his wheezing steed and approached the man. "What else can you tell us, friend?" he said.

The man was still shaking from what he had seen. "Just as the pirate boats made for their ship, I saw someone leap into the water and swim after them," he said. "It was Señor Zorro."

Don Audre gripped the man tightly by the arm. "Did you see him return?" he asked.

The man shook his head. "No. He went into the sea and did not come back. I watched as the pirate craft sailed south."

"My thanks," Don Audre said and gave the man three gold coins for his help. He quickly remounted and turned to his anxious friends. "Then Zorro is on board the pirate ship," he said as he spurred his horse. "We must find a ship and follow."

"There is a trading ship anchored one mile away," the man shouted after the caballeros. "You will see it over that hill."

The caballeros rode away in a cloud of dust. "If the pirate craft is heading south, that means their hidden rendezvous is down the coast," Don Audre said to the men closest to him.

No sooner had he spoken when another cloud of dust appeared. It was a rider galloping full speed after them. The caballeros drew their swords and waited.

The reckless rider was Sergeant Garcia. "Señors!" he shouted. "I have caught up with you at last."

"Have you news?" Don Audre said, signaling to his friends to put away their swords.

"I was hoping to get the same from you," the sergeant said. "When I returned to Reina de los Angeles, I learned of the pirate raid. Captain Ramon was not around, so I ordered myself to catch the scoundrels. What are we waiting for? Forward!"

Don Audre shook his head. "Are you presuming to take command, Sergeant?" he said. "This is a private expedition and these are gentlemen—"

Sergeant Garcia went for his sword. "Are you saying I am not worthy to join in the hunt for my good friend Zorro?" he said angrily. "If so, you must stop me with your sword."

Don Audre cautioned the sergeant to be calm. "We have no love for the governor's soldiers, Sergeant," he said. "But I apologize. You are a friend of our brave companion, Zorro, and so you are one of us. Let's ride!"

The small band of adventurers rode swiftly down the slope to the beach. A short distance away, bobbing on the gentle sea, was the trading schooner. As the men dismounted, another rider appeared out of the darkness. It was Friar Felipe.

"We left you in town," Don Audre said to the old priest. "What are you doing here?"

"I found a horse and came directly," the gentle friar said. His voice changed to anger. "They have taken the precious señorita whom I have known since she was a baby. I was to have married her to my good friend Don Diego today. And to increase my anger, the scoundrels took the sacred goblet from my church. For that affront I have made a vow never to return until I recover it."

"Then you will join us?" Don Audre said.

"Yes," the friar said. "I am ready to follow you."

Don Audre stood in his saddle and waved to his men to follow. "Then to the ship, my brave companions. We have a task before us!"

"The trading schooner has lowered a boat," Sergeant Garcia said as the men dismounted from their tired horses.

A small craft neared the shore. When it landed, a half dozen men climbed from it and carefully approached the armed caballeros, not knowing who they were. Don Audre and the round-bellied friar at his side raised their hands in peace.

"Greetings, Señores," the captain said, studying the two men and their armed companions. "You are Friar Felipe, are you not? And you, Don Audre Ruiz, I know your father well. And what of these caballeros? Are you here to buy from my stock of fine goods?"

Don Audre Ruiz quickly explained the situation. "We need your ship to pursue to pirate craft," he said.

"Pirates?" the captain said in surprise. "You tell me there are pirates in these waters?"

"Sí!" Don Audre said. "Last night they raided Reina de los Angeles and the Pulido hacienda. They robbed the people and stole Señorita Lolita, who was to wed our good friend Don Diego this very day."

The captain of the trading schooner wrinkled his brow. "By the saints," he said. "What are we to do?"

"The scum have sailed toward the south," Don Audre replied. "But with a ship such as yours, we can catch them."

"How many of the rascals are there?" the captain asked.

"Not more than fourscore, as nearly as we can judge," Don Audre said. "But here are twenty bold caballeros, and we are ready to fight."

The schooner captain drew a deep breath as he carefully thought over the matter. "Señors," he said, a moment later, "my ship and my crew are yours to command. We will do anything to rid the seas of such vermin."

The captain signaled his ship with the wave of a torch taken from one of his men. At the command, more small boats were lowered to fetch the band of caballeros, the friar, and Sergeant Garcia from the shore.

Soon the men were aboard the boats, heading for the trading schooner bobbing on the sea. Friar Felipe and Sergeant Garcia sat side by side in one of them. The sergeant stared at the balding priest for a moment.

"Never did I think to join hands with you, Friar Felipe," the sergeant said. "If I am not mistaken, it was you who scolded my men for drinking too much wine at the inn."

The friar nodded his head. "It is true," he said. "But pirates' raids cause rescue parties, and rescue parties cause strange comrades."

The sergeant slapped his knee. "You speak the truth," he said with laughter in his voice. Then his face turned grim. "Is it true they have stolen your sacred goblet?"

Friar Felipe nodded.

The portly sergeant stood on shaky legs as the boat rocked beneath him. "Steal church goblets and brides, do they?" he bellowed. "After I have annihilated the pirates with my blade and rescued the fair señorita, I will regain your goblet as well."

The sergeant's bragging did not escape the patient friar. "If your sword arm is half as strong as your tongue, the pirates are as good as dead already," he said.

The sergeant sat down quickly to avoid falling into the sea. "How is it I must take such insults?" he wailed. "When one of these fine gentlemen insults me, they refuse to fight because they have such noble blood in their veins, they say. And when a friar insults me, I cannot fight because he wears the frock of the church." He turned his gaze toward the dark sea, and his lips curled into a smile. "Ha!" he exclaimed. "I shall have my revenge when I meet up with those scoundrels called pirates. My blade will speak for me then."

Friar Felipe saw that the sergeant's pride was hurt. His eyes twinkled as he reached out to touch the soldier's arm. "We are both needed in this world," the friar said calmly. "There are times when a brave and daring soldier like you should be gentle, and when a man of peace like me must fight."

"You are a noble fellow after all," Sergeant Garcia declared. "I forgive you for scolding me and my men." He gripped his sword tightly. "And when the fight begins, get behind me so I can protect you."

"Thank you," Friar Felipe said. "And my prayers shall shield you in return."

The boat bumped against the schooner, and everyone quickly clambered aboard. The captain began shouting orders the minute his boots hit the deck. Sails dropped from the rigging and filled with wind. The anchor rose from the sea on its stout chain. The bow turned, and the chase was resumed.

Soon the swift schooner was speeding south. The caballeros and crew swept the sea with sharp eyes, eager to spot the pirates' dark sail. A sudden cry directed everyone's attention to a speck in the distance. "A sail!" the lookout shouted. The ship changed course in hot pursuit.

Don Audre studied the pirate ship, which was clearly identified by the black flag of skulls and crossbones flying from her mast. "If Zorro is aboard that foul craft, we must tell him we are near," he said.

The captain agreed. He called to his sailmaster. "Raise a fresh sail," he ordered, "but not before painting the good sign of Zorro on it for all to see."

The bold Z of Zorro was brushed in bold red strokes across a white sail and raised into the wind. Don Audre watched with approval. "Do you think we can overtake the pirate ship?" he asked the captain.

"Courage and swift work does it," the captain said. "We are greatly outnumbered, but my crew has dealt with pirates before. With your friends at our side, we'll fight well." He put his hand on the sturdy wooden rail at his side. "As for my ship's speed, it is but a question of time before we overtake them. We'll be there soon."

Don Audre raised a spyglass to his eye and frowned. "We may be too late. Someone is fighting the entire pirate crew," he said. "Even Zorro cannot fend off fourscore scum."

Sergeant Garcia, standing nearby, heard Don Audre's grim report. "Meal mush and nonsense," he said, drawing his broad cutlass from its sheath and waving it overhead. "That for a pirate . . . and that for another." The thick blade chopped the air filled with imaginary pirates.

Don Audre smiled, but his eyes remained solemn. "Save your strength and your breath," he advised the bold sergeant. "You may need them both soon enough."

Suddenly, a grim scene taking place on the pirate ship silenced everyone on the schooner. "By the saints!" Don Audre exclaimed. "They are making some poor devil walk the plank . . ." His clenched fist flew to his chest. "'Tis Zorro!" he gasped.

"And the little señorita is at the rail, forced to watch him die," Sergeant Garcia said.

The caballeros and the ship's crew stood in horrified silence. Every eye was fixed on the figure who stood on the slim plank jutting out over the sea. The man stood straight and proud, defiantly facing the dark sea. Then, as a cry of rage rose from the throats of those forced to witness the cruel act, he dropped from sight.

Don Audre Ruiz turned away, unable to bear the sight. "He is gone," he said, emotion choking his speech. "Our dear friend Zorro is no more. We can only avenge him now."

The men on the trading schooner gathered around Don Audre. "Save your prayers and your strength for when we board that foul craft," Don Audre said. He clenched his sword tightly and raised it over his head. "Dios! Give strength to my arm!"

Aboard the pirate ship Zorro smiled into the face of death as he stood on the narrow plank. He could not reveal his true feelings because his beloved Lolita, herself bound and a prisoner of the evil Bardoso, was already suffering over his fate.

Zorro was not afraid of death. But knowing what he must leave behind when his body dropped into the sea hurt him deeply. Zorro would die, and with him, Don Diego, though no one knew his secret. His precious bride to be, his friends, his father, his grand estate—he would leave them all for the Great Unknown. But worse, he would be leaving the señorita in grave danger. His only hope was that his friends on the fast-approaching schooner would save her, and avenge him.

A mocking laugh filled the strangely silent deck where the pirates waited for Zorro's plunge. It was Bardoso. "Give him to the sea!" the pirate captain ordered.

The plank was tipped. Zorro stumbled forward. The heavy weight tied to his wrists tugged at him. He knew it would drag him swiftly into the dark depths. His mind glimpsed what was in store. There would be a brief and useless struggle, a moment of wide-eyed horror, and then—the end.

Zorro's eyes met those of the señorita's once more. Their thoughts leaped the empty space separating them as the plank tipped, and the brave caballero shot downward.

There was a sudden splash of cold water, then everything turned black as the waves closed over Zorro's head. He was a powerful swimmer, but not even he could swim with a heavy metal bar tied to wrists lashed behind his back.

Zorro had filled his lungs to bursting just before he hit the water. His legs and arms were already working as he sank swiftly toward the bottom. He jerked his wrists from side to side, expelling precious air in tiny bits as he worked to free himself. Each second dragged him deeper and deeper.

Flashes of red flickered before Zorro's eyes. Like scenes in a dream, he saw the faces of his many friends. Half his life passed before him in his steady downward plunge. The end was painfully near. If this be death, he thought, still tugging at his bonds, unwilling to give up, if this be death then . . .

Hope returned. A final tug at the rope around his wrists brought victory. The thick manila cord was loose! Perhaps the man who bound the heavy weight had not done his work well. Perhaps he secretly admired Zorro for offering to battle the whole pirate crew for his freedom. Whatever the reason, the rope began to slip.

Suddenly the weight fell away. Though the ropes holding his wrists together were still there, the weight was gone! Zorro thrashed his legs fiercely, kicking for the surface. The last of his air was gone. His lungs were empty, burning like fire, and his ears were ringing with the sound of inevitable doom. He was barely conscious as his eyes gazed up through the blanket of water that covered him. Just as they were about to close for the last time, he saw light.

The surface! he thought. With a final, desperate kick he reached the top of the waves. Cool sea air filled his screaming lungs. He was alive.

Still bound at the wrists, Zorro floated in silence as his full senses were gradually restored.

The pirate ship was some distance away, sailing off before a gentle breeze. Zorro saw her crew rushing around the deck, but he could not guess the cause. A wave lifted him high into the air and the pirates' frantic activity suddenly became clear. The trading schooner was overtaking the pirate ship. And Zorro floated helplessly in her path.

Zorro called to the men on the schooner, but they neither saw nor heard him as they prepared for the upcoming battle. He kicked desperately to get out of the way of the sharp hull. The ship's bow wave caught him and swirled him around like a helpless cork. Am I saved from drowning only to be crushed by the ship bearing my friends? he thought.

The vessel loomed over him like a giant wooden cloud. It began to drop as the wave carrying it fell. A loop of anchor chain swayed loosely above him. It splashed into the wave he rode and in that brief instant he threw his leg up, catching hold just before it rose out of the sea again. But he was on it!

Zorro fought to hold on as the ship bore him away. He bobbled on his precarious perch. It would be a task for an athlete with hands unbound, but he refused to let go.

Clinging like a bit of cast-off seaweed to the chain, Zorro pitched up and down as the ship closed the distance between it and the pirate craft. A sharp pain drew his attention. His arm was brushing against the ragged edge of an imperfect link of chain. Hope filled him once more. He dragged the ropes binding his wrists back and forth over the sharp edge, sawing steadily until they parted at last.

The two ships were closing fast. Zorro's legs ached. His arms pulsed with pain and his head pounded. But the thought of fighting with his companions when the two ships clashed urged him on.

Zorro began the painful climb up the chain to the ship's rail. Only when he was safely on the schooner's deck could he relax. A few feet at a time was all he could manage on the perilously swinging anchor chain, but courage gave him strength.

The voices above him added to his determination. On the deck, just a few feet away, Don Audre Ruiz shouted instructions as the caballeros prepared to overtake the pirate ship.

Zorro climbed off the chain and rested for a moment on the butt of the bowsprit. He was weak, but one more step would put him safely on the deck. His hand went for his sword to prepare for the fight. The two ships were perilously close together.

The helmsman on the schooner spun the wheel to put the ship into a position of advantage. The jib over Zorro's head filled with a fresh wind, flapping angrily as the ship turned.

At that instant Don Audre Ruiz saw his friend. "Zorro!" he screamed. But the warning was too late.

The heavy, flapping canvas reached out for the bold caballero perched dangerously on the ship's pitching bow.

Bardoso, too, saw Zorro from the deck of his own ship, now only yards away from the trading schooner. And Sanchez, at his side, certain he was seeing a ghost, gaped in terror.

The jib flapped again. It struck Zorro a sound blow and flicked him from his feeble perch back into the sea!

Don Audre Ruiz and the caballeros had seen Zorro walk the plank. When Don Audre saw Zorro on the bow of the trading schooner he was certain it was his spirit, returned to give courage to the caballeros. "The spirit of Zorro fights with us," he shouted as the ships crashed together with a thunderous roar.

Sanchez, seeing Zorro, had spread the word among the pirates that a ghost had returned against them. When the ships clashed the pirates were strangely quiet. They did not rush forward in their usual manner. Fear froze them in their tracks.

"By my sword, this Zorro must be a demon!" Bardoso screeched, enraged that his men would not fight.

"It's no use," Sanchez cried. "We cannot fight a ghost."

The two ships were locked together, but now Bardoso wanted nothing more than to get away. He was not afraid of the caballeros, but he did fear the supernatural. He shouted commands to steer the pirate craft away from the schooner so the caballeros could not board her.

The foul craft fell away slowly as the helmsman worked frantically to bring her into the wind. Helpless to stop her, the caballeros watched as the ships parted.

Bardoso howled more commands. "Fireballs," he shouted, and from the pirate ship flew a rain of burning pitch and flaming torches. It was a favorite trick of pirates to escape in clouds of smoke.

The caballeros gasped for air as they fought the scores of small fires breaking out on their ship. For many long minutes smoke obscured everything. When it cleared, the pirate ship was well clear and on its way to safety.

"She's running from us!" Don Audre shouted. But the immediate danger of fire at sea, far more deadly than pirates, was of greater concern. Crew and caballeros alike fought desperately to save their ship.

When the fires were extinguished and the smoke had cleared away, a quick inventory was taken. The ship had sustained very little damage. Burned sails were quickly taken down and replaced by spares.

"Do not despair, señor," the captain said to Don Audre Ruiz. "That devil craft will not get far before we are on her heels again." He scratched his head in puzzlement. "I cannot understand their behavior. To a man they acted as if they had seen a ghost."

"And so did I," Don Audre said quietly. "I swear that for an instant I saw Señor Zorro standing at the butt of the bowsprit—and then he was gone."

Soon the new sails were set and filled with currents of wind. The schooner sailed in the wake of the pirate craft once more, vengeance delayed but not forgotten.

Zorro bobbed in the sea, adrift and alone, watching the schooner grow smaller and smaller. The two ships were pulling away. The fires on the schooner were extinguished. New sails had been raised.

Zorro's friends had not abandoned the señorita. He was grateful for that, though he knew it meant his own chances to survive were slim.

A strong tide was running now, and he knew he was too weak to fight it. A spar torn away when the ships crashed drifted nearby. He reached it and painfully drew himself up onto it, exhausted.

Zorro gazed across the sea. A dirty streak on the horizon was the land he would have to reach. He took stock of his predicament. His wrists were raw and bleeding and his leg, aching. The glare of the sun on the water nearly blinded him. Hunger and thirst added to the torture. He put his hand to his side to make sure his faithful blade was still there. He smiled grimly. "Sword of Zorro," he said, "we are in a sorry state. This is a trial such as we have never faced before. But we must win through." His heart pumped courage through his aching body, and he raised his voice in song. "*Atención*! A caballero's near—"

But his voice broke. The ships were tiny specks on the horizon. Land was equally far away. "It is a waste to sing when I need my precious energy to save myself," he said. He slipped into the water and, still clinging to the spar, began to swim for land.

Zorro swam for hours. The spar slowed his progress, but without it he would have nothing to rest on when weakness overcame him. On and on he forced the spar through the water, unable to tell if he was getting closer to land or not. The thought of a powerful current sweeping him farther out to sea plagued him. Pain very nearly forced him to quit. As the sun began to sink, his spirits too slipped lower.

Zorro's muscles acted mechanically. His mind rambled out of control. He would find himself giving up, then the thought of Señorita Lolita would revive him and he'd swim on.

Twilight came, and then darkness. A pale moon rose over the black sea. On through the night the weary caballero swam for an unseen shore. His mind began to play tricks. He imagined a band of pirates pursuing him. Then the face of the pretty señorita would banish the pirates. Saltwater burned his throat. Unendurable weakness signaled that the end was near. Lolita's image hung above the sea like a taunting spirit. "*Atención*! A caballero's near—" he tried to sing but it was no use. "Must rest," he gasped. Then, with dark water lapping at his face and his aching arms losing their grip on the thick wooden spar, he passed into unconsciousness.

Hideous dreams filled Zorro's mind, and a roar of thunder filled his ears. His fingers let loose of the spar. The brave caballero slipped into the sea. As the water closed around his head he thought he heard a distant voice calling to him as if to calm him.

"Señor! Señor!" the voice within his head said.

Zorro's sunburned eyes opened expecting to view eternity. But the sound of nearby surf said he was wrong. Something touched his lips, and cool, pure water poured down his parched throat.

"Señor!" the eerie inner voice repeated. "For the love of the saints, come back to life!"

Zorro sat up. He was in a native hut not far from the sea, on a sandy beach. A man held him with an arm beneath his shoulders so he could drink. "Ha!" Zorro gasped, realizing he had been saved. "Who are you that I owe you my life?"

The man did not answer. Instead he put his finger to his lips and shook his head slowly from side to side.

Zorro believed the man cautioned silence. "Is there danger nearby?" he asked.

The man smiled calmly, then repeated the gesture with his finger to his lips.

For a moment Zorro was puzzled. Then he understood. "You are mute," he said. "You cannot speak."

The man nodded.

"But you hear my words?"

The man nodded again.

Zorro clasped the man's arm. "I have found a friend," he said. "I can never repay you for my life, though somehow I will try."

The man smiled warmly. He was a handsome fellow with a face that spoke of hidden wisdom. He made Zorro comfortable on a simple cot near the open door of the hut. He pointed to the sea a short distance away. The broken spar lay on the beach.

"You found me drifting on that piece of wreckage?" Zorro asked. "When?"

The man knelt to the ground. With his finger he traced a circle in the dust with rays extending from its rim.

"The sun?" Zorro said.

The man nodded.

"How many?"

The man raised one finger.

"I have been here for a whole day?" Zorro exclaimed.

The man nodded vigorously.

Zorro leaned over the edge of the cot and drew an irregular line in the dust. "This is the coast of California," he said. He drew an X near the line. "This is Reina de los Angeles." He drew yet another line, which connected to the X. "And this is El Camino Real." He looked into the man's eyes to make certain he understood. "Show me where we are."

The man placed his fingertip on the crude map at a point on the coast below Reina de los Angeles.

Zorro drank more water. His wits were returning fast. He looked around the hut. It was clearly the home of a very poor man. Outside the door was a small boat filled with lines and nets. "You are a fisherman?" Zorro asked.

The man nodded.

"Has this always been your life?"

The man's face darkened as unseen memories bubbled behind his piercing eyes. He shook his head violently. Without waiting for another question, he traced the outline of a fine hacienda in the dust and then pointed to his chest.

"You owned land and a fine house?" Zorro asked with surprise. "What happened?"

The man placed his finger on Zorro's rough map and drew another X up the coast from Reina de los Angeles.

"San Francisco!" Zorro exclaimed. "The home of the governor?"

The man wiped away the X in the dust as if he would like to crush what it stood for.

"So it was the governor's taxes that took your home," Zorro said with understanding.

The man put his finger to his mouth.

"And your tongue! The beast! And I thought it a cruel fate to fall into the hands of mere pirates," Zorro said.

At the word *pirates* the man drew another mark on the dirt map, a skull and crossbones.

"A pirate camp is nearby?" Zorro shouted.

The man nodded vigorously. He held up nine fingers and then proceeded to draw a sketch of huts and women and children.

Zorro studied the picture before him. "So the pirates' camp is nine miles from here."

The man hurried to a small fire and returned with a plate of steaming beans and rice. He gave it to Zorro who ate eagerly.

"I must go to the pirate camp as soon as I have my strength." Zorro looked deep into the man's eyes. "You will be rewarded," he said. "I have a friend in Reina de los Angeles. He is Don Diego Vega. Go to him in a week's time and he will pay you—"

The man smiled warmly as he shook his head slowly back and forth. He placed his hand in his shirt and pulled out a length of black silk, which he handed to Zorro.

Zorro's hand flashed to his face. It was bare. The mask was gone. "Then you know who I am?" he said softly.

The man said nothing. He drew the figure of a man in the dust. Under it he wrote the initials DV.

"Diego Vega," Zorro said.

The man nodded. Then he added another initial alongside the first. It was the bold slashing Z, the sign of Zorro.

Before Zorro could speak the man put one hand to his lips and the other to his heart as he shook his head sharply back and forth.

"My secret is safe with you," Zorro said as he affixed his mask. "I know in my heart you will guard it with your life."

The men solemnly shook hands.

Zorro looked into the man's dark eyes. "You know both of my names," he said, "yet I know not yours. How are you called?"

The man placed his finger on the ground and wrote his name boldly in the dust—Bernardo.

SEVEN

∽

The Ghost Returns

Bardoso watched as the trading schooner set new sails and continued the pursuit. Though he knew his men outnumbered the caballeros and crew on the schooner, something told him to avoid a fight. "We'll lose that sorry craft," he said. "Then we'll go to the rendezvous to divide the loot and turn the señorita over to the man who comes to claim her. If they still follow, we'll fight the caballeros on land. The ghost of a man drowned at sea is powerless on land, so I have heard."

Sanchez was still shaking like a child. "It is not my mind to fight ghosts," he said. "We are bedeviled for some reason."

Bardoso descended to the cabin where Señorita Lolita remained a prisoner.

The young girl had fainted when Zorro had plunged into the sea. Sanchez had carried her to her small cell. Now she sat up with a start as Bardoso entered. Her hand went secretly to the dagger at her side.

"So you have recovered your right mind, eh?" Bardoso asked. "It's just as well you make the best of it. We are running away from your friends. There is no hope of rescue. Perchance the man we have stolen you for will be kind."

Fire flashed in the señorita's eyes. "Foul beast," she said. "What kind of honor is it for twenty men to take one girl captive, to strike down my father, to burn my home, and then to send my protector to an early grave?"

"There are other men to protect you, and other homes," Bardoso said. "And it was Sanchez, not I, who struck your father. Anyway, it was not fatal."

"You are their chief," Lolita shouted. "You are the one responsible. You are nothing more than a beast."

Bardoso shrugged. "Words do not hurt my tough hide," he said. "Now, for you it is best to be calm."

Señorita Lolita raised herself from the bunk and staggered toward the thick-chested pirate chief. "How can I be calm when there is no future for me save dishonor or death?" she said through trembling lips. "When the moment comes, it will not take me long to choose."

"When the moment comes, you'll change your mind," Bardoso said.

"Never," Lolita spat. Her mind turned to Zorro. "He whom you sent to death in the sea is worth tenscore of you, and his friends who follow you tenscore more. Do you think you can escape them forever?"

"I shall wipe them from the face of the earth," Bardoso bragged.

"Not while the memory of the one I love is alive in my heart," Lolita vowed. "You have killed him and so now you will pay—" The girl's small hand flew to her breast and drew forth the dagger. With a cry of rage she struck out wildly at the pirate chief.

Bardoso was taken by surprise. He lurched quickly to one side, but the blade struck his arm, tearing his flesh and drawing blood. "By my naked blade!" he swore.

Lolita lunged at him again, but this time he was ready. He tore the dagger from her hand and tossed her on the bunk.

Certain the enraged pirate would make an end of her, the girl braced herself. But the pirate did not move. Instead, he merely slipped the dagger into his belt and, glancing lightly at his wounded arm, stepped to the door.

"A maid with spirit, eh?" he said. "I am grateful I am not this Captain Ramon who will have to tame you. Glad I will be when I turn you over to him." He exited the cell-like room, but before closing the heavy door, spoke again. "I have enough battles on my hands without fighting the likes of you. I'll send a man with food. Such a warrior as yourself needs to conserve her strength." He laughed, then slammed the door shut, throwing the heavy bar into place.

Lolita collapsed onto the bunk, her strength giving way to tears. "Oh, Zorro," she cried. She put her head on her arm and sobbed for a man she was sure was dead.

The pirate ship sailed back and forth across the open seas vainly trying to shake off the schooner that dogged its wake. But it was useless. The white-sailed vessel was constantly in sight. Bardoso cursed the bright moon that blanketed the water with light, revealing his every move.

Each time Bardoso tried a new tack, even in the hour of greatest darkness before dawn, the schooner stayed with him. The pirate chief was determined to shake his pursuers before heading back for his lair so they would not find it, but nothing he could do worked. At last he gave up. He knew he would have to fight the caballeros eventually. Once or twice he felt like turning, to attack the ship at sea. Each time the thought of the ghost of Zorro deterred him. "A sea ghost cannot fight on land," he muttered. "On land I will have them at my mercy." And so he headed for the rendezvous.

It was almost nightfall when the pirate craft headed into the small bay that was their home port. The schooner was a few miles behind.

The pirate ship lowered its sails and dropped anchor. There would be time to prepare for the arrival of the schooner.

Fires burned onshore. Women and children tended them, waiting for the small boats to carry the pirates to the wide beach. Bardoso was in the first boat to land. The moment his feet touched solid ground, he began shouting orders.

Guards were posted on three sides of the pirate camp. The ship was brought closer to shore so it could be defended easily. When the preparations on land were done, Bardoso returned to his ship for the young señorita. As he crossed the deck, he saw the schooner sailing toward the bay. Then it turned and headed back out to sea.

As Bardoso watched, Sanchez bound Lolita's wrists behind her back. "You go ashore, wench," the pirate chief said. "There you will be held until Captain Ramon comes to claim you, though why he should want a spitfire like you I can't understand."

The women and children onshore jeered at Lolita when she stepped onto shore from the small boat. The pirate chief took her to a large adobe building, the best structure in the camp, and thrust her inside.

A woman tending a fire nearby followed Bardoso and his beautiful prisoner into the building. "So, a younger, prettier woman, is it?" she said, her eyes flaming.

Bardoso turned to the woman. "She is a share of the loot, Inez," he said.

The woman pointed a sharp finger at Bardoso. "So, it has come at last, eh? I am to be tossed aside for a comely maid stolen from some rich hacienda."

Bardoso stood back on his heels. "You are foolish to be jealous, Inez. Do you think you hold my love for life?"

Inez, her own beauty a thing of the past, struck out at Lolita's face but the pirate chief seized her wrists.

"Peace!" he bellowed. "I want none of the wench. She is not my share of the loot. She was stolen for a great man who will come to claim her."

"Is this the truth?" Inez asked.

"It is," Bardoso thundered. "Now put her into the storeroom. Feed her well. Treat her gently. She is not to be harmed." He glanced over his shoulder toward the dark sea. The schooner could not be seen, but he knew it was out there.

"We were followed," the pirate continued. "A schooner full of caballeros would rescue her. She must not be rescued!"

The older woman grinned. Secure that she was not being replaced by the pretty señorita, she bid the young girl to enter the storeroom.

Bardoso hurried outside. The night was black but the moon was shining. He made the rounds of his guards who stood watch over the camp. They were ready for an attack. But there would be no attack this night.

The schooner was safely anchored two miles down the coast. On its quietly bobbing deck, Don Audre Ruiz and the captain made plans.

"I know the place," the captain said. "I once put in there during a storm. The land is open. It will be impossible for us to make a surprise attack."

"Then what is your advice?" Don Audre Ruiz asked.

The captain whispered, as if his voice could somehow be carried on the breeze to the pirate lair. "I will put you and your caballeros ashore here," he said. "Take them to the pirate camp and wait for dawn. I will take my crew to the other side, to attack from there. I will leave the ship here with enough men to get her to sea if the pirate craft comes after her."

"Agreed," Don Audre said.

"You will be outnumbered four to one," the captain said. "They may have pistols, and the fight will be hand-to-hand."

Don Audre Ruiz drew himself up proudly. "Four beasts to one caballero is an equal fight," he said. "You must remember that Señorita Pulido is their prisoner." He looked to the sea. "And I am not forgetting what they did to my great friend Zorro. We will attack!"

Soon all the men except for a small crew to man the ship were onshore. Don Audre led his caballeros to within a mile of the pirate camp as the captain circled with his men to the opposite side.

The caballeros waited for the dark hour before dawn, resting for what they knew would be a fight for their lives, the life of Señorita Pulido, and the honor of their lost friend Zorro.

Sergeant Garcia approached Don Audre as the time drew near. "I am ready, señor. What are your orders?"

"That every man do his best," Don Audre replied. "The señorita is to be rescued and returned to the schooner."

"And the pirates?" the sergeant asked, grooming the point of his thick blade.

"They chose their fate when they raided La Reina de los Angeles and stole the señorita," Don Audre said. "And they sealed it when they sent Zorro to his early grave."

Sergeant Garcia called for the friar. "Friar Felipe!"

The friar approached. "Señor?"

"You are my friend," Garcia said. "If the fight gets thick, stand behind me that I may protect you. A fight is no place for a friar."

The friar nodded. "Perhaps," he said. "But there is the matter of the goblet."

The sergeant puffed up his chest. "By the saints, I take it upon myself to get the goblet for you."

"Do so and I shall call you son," the friar said.

The sergeant bowed his head for a moment. "I have been an evil man in my time," he said. "But I trust this day will make up for it." He turned to the leader of the caballeros. "Don Audre, I am ready!"

Don Audre Ruiz led the way along the shore toward the pirate camp. When the band of men reached the crest of a slope, they saw the camp below, washed in the first rays of the morning sun.

There were many more pirates than Don Audre expected. To do battle seemed like a hopeless task.

The men looked at one another. They were still dressed in their fine silks and satins, with jeweled swords at their sides. The pirates, ready for a fight in their stronghold, were ragged and dirty.

"If only Zorro were here to lead us," Don Audre Ruiz said with a sigh. "But he is not. Let us not forget why he is missing and strike all the harder for what the pirates have done to him." He whipped out his gleaming sword and waved it high over his head. "Are you ready?" he said to his men.

The caballeros drew their blades and shouted their answer with cheers.

With Don Audre Ruiz at the head of a perfect line, the caballeros moved slowly and carefully to attack. To inspire his men and give them courage, Don Audre began a lusty song of old:

"Singing caballeros, going forth to die!
Laughing in the face of grinning Death!
Facing a task that's hopeless, ready yet to try!
Singing with the last of earthly breath!"

The caballeros joined in, their voices ringing across the land and sea. When the song ended, they were ready. And as they could see, so were the pirates. The clash would come in a very few minutes.

Suddenly, from the distant top of a small slope between the two attacking forces, another song was raised.

"*Atención!* A caballero's near—!"

The caballeros looked at one another with astonishment. Running down the slope toward them was a figure they knew well. Don Audre Ruiz gave a great cry of joy and the caballeros cheered.

"Zorro!" they cried. "Zorro!" And they rushed to the attack.

The pirates had decided to make the fight away from their huts so they rushed forward, shrieking battle cries and brandishing their weapons.

The caballeros advanced in a perfect line, their blades held ready as Zorro hurried down the slope to join them, still singing and shouting.

The pirates had few firearms and little ammunition, while the caballeros had only their swords. Coming directly from the elegant bachelor supper, they had worn no pistols.

The pirates opened fire on the advancing caballeros. There was a moment of silence when the roar of the guns died away. Then the battle was joined in hand-to-hand combat.

The line of caballeros was broken, and each man found himself in a duel with three or more pirates. They fought bravely, sometimes shouting encouragement to one another, sometimes in silence, feeling they were doomed. But they fought on, determined to do what they could before the battle went against them.

At the moment when things looked grimmest, a loud noise went up from the opposite side of the pirate camp. The crew of the trading schooner, led by the captain, attacked.

For a moment the battle favored the men from the schooner, but Bardoso had men in reserve who poured into the fight.

Zorro reached the bottom of the slope and instantly joined his friends. With flashing sword he desperately tried to turn the tide of battle. "At the scum, caballeros!" he shouted over the bedlam. "They cannot stand against us."

Sergeant Garcia saw Zorro. "To me, Señor Zorro," he roared as he held off two pirates with his flashing sword. "We'll carve a pathway through these swine."

But Zorro didn't hear him. He had seen his old friend Don Audre Ruiz fighting for his life, and he quickly fought his way to his side. His sword cut the air so swiftly it seemed he carried ten blades. One of the pirates fell, but Zorro pressed on like a man possessed, rushing straight at the pirates at the head of the battle. His voice sent a chilling note over the tumult. "Atención! A caballero's near—!"

A pirate froze in his tracks at the sound. "The ghost," he shrieked. "It is the ghost from the sea!"

Bardoso whirled around as Sanchez, a look of terror on his face, turned to retreat. He saw Zorro. "It is no ghost, you sons of dogs," he screamed at his men. "It is Zorro, saved from the sea. Get him! Bring him to me alive."

The pirates paused, uncertain if it were a man or a ghost standing before them. Bardoso shouted to his men again. "Does the sword of a ghost run red with blood?" he taunted.

The pirate chief's words made sense, and his men gathered their courage and surged forward again. The caballeros' line was broken once more and they began to scatter.

Zorro and Don Audre Ruiz fought side by side as well as they could but in the open could not protect their backs and so were circled by a howling band of foes.

The fight swirled around the two friends, and both knew their fine display of courage and swordsmanship was not winning the battle. Slowly the pirates were traveling the road to triumph.

Zorro knew he could not give up. He could not recklessly throw his life away as long as the señorita was a prisoner. He would have to live if he hoped to rescue her. He glanced around. Half of the caballeros were wounded and still more pirates poured forth. The end was near.

Then a new menace came from the corral where the fine horses stolen from the caballeros by the pirates were kept. Terrified by the noise of battle, they broke down the fence and rushed through the fighting men, knocking down pirates and caballeros alike in their wild charge.

A lone stallion crashed between Zorro, Don Audre Ruiz, and the fierce men fighting them. It broke off the fight, but it separated Zorro from Don Audre as well. Now each man was alone, to fight his own fight against the closing circle of pirates.

"Take them alive!" Bardoso screamed above the tumult. "They will bring a rich ransom or be tortured. Take them alive."

Zorro and his friends understood. If they were captured, they would be held for ransom. But if the ransom were not paid quickly enough, they would be tortured. The caballeros fought like madmen. They knew that even though they could not win, they dared not lose.

"Get Zorro," Bardoso commanded. "A rich reward to the man who brings him to me. And this time I'll make him a ghost for sure."

For a moment Zorro and Don Audre Ruiz were fighting side by side again. "Audre!" Zorro shouted to his friend. "Can you win free of the dogs?"

"I am surrounded," Don Audre called back.

"One of us must break free," Zorro cried. "There is the señorita—"

"Get away," Don Audre Ruiz shouted. "Save her. And the saints bless you—"

Zorro steeled himself for what he must do. "I will return," he shouted to Don Audre. "It is a promise. But let them take you. Alive you have hope. Dead, you are gone forever."

There was no time to hear the reply from Don Audre Ruiz. Two eager pirates determined to earn the reward for his capture advanced on Zorro.

Zorro hurled himself forward, his blade slicing the air. One pirate fell. The other ran in fear. Others took their places, and he fought desperately to free a path through them. He glanced back at his friend and caught a glimpse of Don Audre Ruiz being disarmed.

The largest of the stallions, still frightened by the sounds of battle, rushed toward Zorro. One man stood between the bold caballero and the horse. Zorro's blade cut the air; the pirate jumped aside in terror. The horse hurtled by. And in the moment of his passing, Zorro leaped onto the animal's bare back.

The giant creature hesitated. Zorro kicked its broad flanks with his spurs. The horse reared high above the advancing pirates, tumbling them over like sticks of wood, and then galloped through them.

The horse dashed up the slope, carrying Zorro out of the pitch of battle, a battle already drawing to a sorry close for the caballeros. Zorro, his eyes burning with anger at the sight, forced the horse to turn and in a bold ride through the pirate band sent them running for their lives. He grabbed one pirate by the collar and lifted him high into the air before tossing him back like a bag of sand. He tugged at the horse's mane to ride through the band again, but this time the horse's fear could not be governed. And so, riding straight and tall on the hurtling beast's broad back, Zorro rode up the slope and away from the pirate camp.

Bardoso stared at the cloud of dust that was all that remained of his prisoner. Furious, he cursed the bold caballero. And Zorro answered the pirate chief's oath with a burst of song: "*Atención!* A caballero's near . . . "

EIGHT

∽

A Turn of Fate

Señorita Lolita Pulido walked into the storeroom of the adobe building with her head held high and a look of defiant pride on her face. But when the heavy door closed behind her, she buried her face in her hands and dropped to a stool where she listened.

Bardoso and his woman Inez were no longer outside the door. There seemed to be no hope left. She believed her protector was at the bottom of the sea. She was in the hands of pirates with no way to escape.

A short while later Inez returned with food and water and a torch that she fastened to the wall, for it was dark in the storeroom. "Eat, wench," she commanded. "And let me warn you it will do you no good to make eyes at my Bardoso."

Lolita drank some water but could not bring herself to try the foul-looking food.

"Too dainty for pirate fare, eh?" Inez sneered, rubbing her fat nose with a forefinger. "You'll eat when you get hungry enough."

Lolita stood and approached Inez. "You are a woman," she said. "Somewhere in your heart there must be sympathy for another woman."

Inez shook her head. "Not much," she answered. "Few women have shown sympathy or kindness toward me. I was a poor girl working on a hacienda. When I gave my love to a handsome traveler, a woman of your class kicked me out."

Lolita sighed. "That is the way of the world," she said. "But still, you must have some pity left. Would you let happen to me what surely will if I cannot avoid it?"

"And what would you have me do?" Inez replied.

"Help me to escape," the señorita begged. "Somehow I will get up El Camino Real to Reina de los Angeles, where I have friends. I will send you money. More than you'll ever get from Captain Ramon, the man who is to have me for his prize."

"Ha!" Inez laughed. "Bardoso would take it from me, and then find another woman. No. I know nothing of business deals with this Captain Ramon. Nor do I care to know them."

"Have you no pity?" Lolita asked.

"I have nothing to do with it," Inez replied. "I have orders to give you food and water, nothing more. That is the end of it."

Before Lolita could speak, the woman left the room, closing the heavy door behind her.

In the flickering torchlight Lolita inspected the dreary room. It was empty except for some old casks that had once contained olives and tallow. There was but one door and only a single window with metal bars.

Escape was impossible, the senorita decided. She buried her face in her hands again, her future now more certain than ever. Exhaustion began to come over her. She curled up in a corner and soon fell asleep.

A roar of men's voices and the clash of steel awakened her. The torch had burned out, but the room was bright with sunlight. She hurried to the small window, which she could reach by standing on an empty cask, and peered out.

The pirate camp was bedlam. Men were arming themselves and rushing about as Bardoso barked orders at them. Then there was a lull and from the distance she heard a song:

"*Atención*! A caballero's near—"

Lolita's heart skipped a beat. But her mind told her she was foolish to hope. Though it was Zorro's song, she knew he was dead at the bottom of the sea. It must be another caballero singing the song, she thought. But it meant Zorro's friends were near and would rescue her.

After another lull the battle began. First there was nothing but the shouts of men, but as the fight entered the open area outside her window, she saw the men from the schooner fighting for their lives. She jumped from the cask, ran to the door, and began pounding on it with her fists. After a time it was opened by Inez.

"What is it, wench?" the woman asked. "More food and water?"

"No," Lolita gasped. "What is going on? There is a fight—"

"A battle," Inez said. "Some caballeros came in a ship and attacked our camp."

"Who is winning?" Lolita asked breathlessly.

Inez scoffed. "The caballeros are outnumbered. We have them four to one. The prisoners will be held for ransom, or tortured. It will be a lesson to gentlemen not to fight with pirates. Gentlemen are only gentlemen, but men are men."

"Gentlemen are always gentlemen," the señorita replied proudly. "But sometimes mere men are beasts."

Inez became angered. "Do you want me to rock your head with a blow, wench?" she said. "Ha! There will be rare sport if this Señor Zorro is taken prisoner."

"Zorro?" Lolita gasped. "But Zorro is dead."

"He may have walked the plank," Inez said, "but somehow he was saved from the sea. He's out there now fighting for his life."

Lolita's heart beat wildly. It *was* Zorro she had heard. But her momentary hope fell away again for she was certain Zorro could not have survived walking the plank with weights fastened to his wrists. The pirate woman was mistaken. The man was someone who looked like Zorro and nothing more.

Certain she was right and that only her own wits would save her, Lolita began to act like she had never acted before in her life. It was an act of desperation.

"So the pirates will win," she said lightly. "And there will be a lot of ransom money and loot."

Inez was confused. "How is this? Now you seem joyful you won't be rescued."

Lolita glanced at Inez. "I am a prisoner, it's true," she said. "But perhaps I'll be more than that soon."

Inez was curious. "What do you mean by that?" she snapped.

"Perhaps I believe as you do that it would be better to have a real man than to wed a gentleman of noble blood," Lolita said. "After all, don't you agree it's interesting Bardoso stole me the night before my wedding?"

"What do you mean by that?"

Lolita smiled. "Did you really believe the story that a Captain Ramon would come for me?" she asked. Then she added quickly, "Of course, I did too, at first. But then I realized the truth. You are getting old—and fat."

Inez turned red with anger. "Wench," she shouted, threatening to strike the defenseless girl.

"If you strike me, Bardoso will punish you," Lolita said.

Inez paused. "Bardoso punish me?" she said. "Ha!"

Lolita cocked her head haughtily. "Are you so easily fooled?" she asked. "I'm not. Bardoso means to keep me for himself. And since escape is impossible, I will make the best of it. If I'm to be the woman of a pirate chief, I must be loyal to him, so why shouldn't I hope he gets a lot of ransom and loot?"

The older woman shook her head. "If I thought this to be the truth—" she said.

Lolita laughed again. "Can't you see that it is?" she asked. "Though Captain Ramon has dealings with Bardoso, the story that I was captured for the captain was nothing more than a falsehood to fool you."

Inez pointed a sharp finger at Lolita. "Ha! So you would take my place, eh?" she cried.

Lolita threw up her hands. Her face filled with compassion. "I have no desire to take your place, but after all, I have no other choice, do I?"

"I could kill you both," Inez said.

Lolita shrugged her shoulders. "Me, perhaps. But him? Never!"

Inez's anger cooled. "You are right," she said.

The young señorita gathered all her wits and courage before she spoke next. "There is a way," she teased.

Inez leaped at the chance. "How is that, wench?" she asked anxiously.

"If you help me to escape, you will have Bardoso to yourself," Lolita said. "You will have time to win back his love before he raids again and finds another to replace you."

"If I help you to escape he will kill me," Inez said.

"Not if it is made to appear that I escaped on my own," Lolita said. "If you break the window so it will look as if I did it, nobody will know you helped."

The woman seemed to be interested. "If I thought for a moment you were speaking the truth—"

Lolita became bold. "Then don't help me and you'll see whether it's the truth."

Inez hesitated. She studied the young girl's face closely. She grunted and hurried out of the room, leaving Lolita to tremble in fear that her gamble had been lost.

Soon Inez returned bearing a strip of heavy iron with a sharp point at one end. "Watch the door," she snapped to Lolita. She began to hack at the masonry holding the window in place.

"Hurry," Lolita said. "I am small and don't need much space—"

"It is already done," Inez crowed.

"I must have some old clothes," Lolita said. "I will leave what I am wearing in return."

The woman was more than eager to trade rags for silk. She left the room again, returning with a tattered, dirty dress for Lolita to wear.

The señorita changed clothes. She rubbed dirt on her face and disarrayed her hair.

Inez stared at the girl's delicate feet. "A woman in rags does not wear fine slippers," she said.

Lolita kicked off her slippers and put her feet into the filthy sandals furnished by the woman. "I am ready," she said, and headed for the window.

"Not that way," Inez said, grasping her by the arm. "There are guards."

Lolita climbed atop the cask and peered out the hole where the window had been. A half dozen men guarded the camp and would see her leave the window.

"Is there no way out?" Lolita cried in despair.

"Only the front," Inez answered. "But women and children have been ordered to remain inside. They will surely notice you."

"They will shout for me to get back inside, but I'll run as if frightened," Lolita said. "You bar the door so when they come to look for me, it will appear that I have escaped through the window."

Inez shook her head. "I'm afraid," she said.

"Aren't you also afraid of another woman taking your place?" Lolita taunted.

Eyes blazing, Inez strode to the door and thrust it open. "The fighting is on the other side," she said. "Now is your chance."

Lolita's heart pounded. This would be her only chance.

"You must hurry," Inez said. "If you are caught you must take all the blame. Bardoso would kill me if he knew."

"Give me a dagger," Lolita begged.

The woman hesitated, then handed the girl a dagger that had been hidden in the folds of her own shawl. Lolita tucked it out of sight. She was ready. The two women looked at one another in silence for a brief instant, then they both made for the door.

But when they reached it, the door flew open as if by itself. Standing on the other side, turning hope to dark despair in an instant, was none other than Captain Ramon!

There was a moment of astonishment as all three stood at the open door. Then Lolita gave a cry of fright and recoiled against the wall. With Zorro dead, the pirates winning the battle against the caballeros, and now faced with the man she both loathed and feared, her future never seemed so dark. "*Dios!*" she exclaimed.

Inez, not knowing who the man was, grabbed the iron bar and raised it against him but he snatched her arm.

"Do not be afraid of me, hag," he said. "For even though I wear the uniform of the governor's troops, I am a good friend of Bardoso. I am Captain Ramon of Reina de los Angeles!"

Inez dropped the bar. "Ha!" she exclaimed. "So you are Captain Ramon." She paused as the noise of the fighting continued. "It must be true or you would not have lived to reach this building. But why are you here?"

"To see the little lady standing behind you," Ramon said, smiling. "I see she has been kept safe."

"You are here to claim her?" Inez asked with a puzzled look.

"Of course," Captain Ramon said. "What else?"

"Ha!" Inez snorted, realizing that she had been tricked into helping Lolita escape. Now she would have to speak quickly to save herself.

"You have arrived just in time," Inez said. "The wench was locked in the storeroom. When I heard no sounds, I opened the door only to find her dressed like this, ready to escape through a hole she made with this iron bar." She waved the bar under the captain's nose. "Had it not been for me, she would be gone."

"You have done well," Ramon declared. Then, turning to Lolita, he said, "You might have been hurt on the outside. It is enough you are dressed in rags unsuited to your station, and have soiled your hands and pretty face."

"Your presence soils me more," Lolita spat.

"You prefer pirates, señorita?" the captain asked.

"They are not the lowest beasts who walk on two legs," Lolita answered.

Ramon laughed. "Such a biting tongue in such a sweet face."

"More biting than your blade," Lolita said. "Why do you not show your true colors and fight alongside your friends, the pirates, against men of gentle blood?"

Captain Ramon bowed in mockery. "If you would glance out the door you will see the fight has ended. The caballeros are now prisoners to be jeered at by the women and children." He turned to Inez. "Go join them. I will guard the señorita well."

The woman shuffled from the building, eager to tell Bardoso how she had prevented the young señorita from escaping as proof of her loyalty and faithfulness.

When she was gone Captain Ramon spoke quickly to Lolita. "Into the storeroom," he commanded. "I wish to close the door so we are not overheard."

"What do you mean?" Lolita said warily.

When they entered the storeroom Captain Ramon hurried to the window and looked out. He had had a two-day ride from Reina de los Angeles to think out the plan he would now unfold.

Captain Ramon was playing a double game. He loved his uniform and the wealth and power that went with it too much to become an outcast—which is what he would have become if it was ever known that he had stolen the señorita. He wished to reinstate himself in the good graces of the caballeros. And he wished to aid his master, the governor, whose credit in the southland was not good these days.

More importantly, Ramon had heard that Zorro had walked the plank. Now he could pursue Lolita openly. He wanted the señorita to believe he was rescuing her in order to win her love. So he pretended to be on her side.

"I am hurt that you speak unkindly of me, señorita," he said, feigning surprise that she did not understand why he was there. "I have risked much to be of service to you."

Lolita jerked back. "Of service to me?" she snapped. "When it was by your orders that I was abducted, my home burned, and my father cut down!"

Now Ramon shuddered with surprise. "Is that what the pirates have told you?" he said. "Listen. It is a game I have been playing with them. I have pretended to be their friend so that the soldiers may have an easy time capturing them later."

"You are playing a game with *me*," the señorita said.

"Oh, no," Ramon lied. "I have pretended to be in league with the pirates. I have followed them here to rescue you. And now that I know you are safe, I shall ride to San Diego de Alcalá, which is only a few miles away, and fetch troopers to rescue you, free the caballeros, and wipe out this nest of pirates!"

Lolita was uncertain, but the story sounded convincing.

"It was the only way, señorita," the devious captain went on. "This has been a trap arranged to capture the pirates."

"I wish I could believe you," Lolita said.

"Believe me, señorita," Captain Ramon pleaded. "I love you so much—"

"I am betrothed," Lolita said quietly.

"If you would live with me—"

"Señor!" Lolita said sharply. "If we must talk, let us talk of other things."

Ramon approached her. "Do you not realize you are in my power?" he asked.

"Now you are showing your true colors," Lolita replied.

"No," Ramon said quickly. "I am showing you I am not taking advantage of this situation. I intend to rescue you and the caballeros, and I am risking my own life to do it. If I succeed, would you perhaps look upon me with some favor?"

Captain Ramon's deceit was so perfectly played that for a moment Lolita thought he spoke the truth. "If I have misjudged you, señor, I am sorry," she said. "But it is useless to ask for more as I am betrothed to Don Diego Vega."

Captain Ramon's eyes were pleading. "If only you could believe me—"

"Perhaps I could," Lolita said, "after you have demonstrated your loyalty."

The captain turned toward the door. "Then I go now to talk with Bardoso and later to San Diego de Alcalá for the troopers. I must pretend I want you guarded until I return."

Captain Ramon left Inez guarding Lolita and hurried from the adobe building. The scene of battle was quiet. The pirates had won. Now they pushed the captured caballeros into another adobe building where they would be imprisoned. Even in defeat the caballeros held their heads high, laughing and jesting with each other.

Ramon forced himself to steady his nerves as he looked for Bardoso. He was playing a hazardous game where one mistake would uncover his deception. He already had Bardoso's confidence. Now he would go to San Diego de Alcalá to lure the troopers there to the pirate camp. Though he would tell Bardoso the plan was for the pirates to ambush the troopers, he meant to have the troopers wipe out the pirate camp. In that way the caballeros and the señorita would be rescued and he, Ramon, would be hailed a hero. This would reinstate him in the good graces of the caballeros and increase his chances of winning Señorita Pulido's hand.

Ramon gloated over his plan. With the pirates wiped out, the governor would reward him by ordering Lolita's father, Don Carlos Pulido, to give the señorita to Ramon in marriage. Don Diego would have no choice but to give up Lolita.

It was a pretty plot by a man who would willingly sell his friends and foes alike to advance his own interests. As the devious captain reveled in his own cleverness, he rounded the corner of a building and walked straight into the burning eyes of Friar Felipe.

"What business does an officer of the governor have in a pirate's den unless he is a prisoner of war?" the friar demanded.

Captain Ramon quickly recovered his composure. "Perhaps there are things you do not understand, friar," he replied with an elegant bow.

"And perhaps, Comandante, there are things that I do understand," the friar said with bitterness in his voice. "Perhaps my years of service in behalf of honest men have taught me to recognize a traitor's face when I see one."

Captain Ramon's eyes narrowed. "You are a friar and wear a gown that requires respect," he said angrily. "But do not tempt me too far. Now say your prayers and leave men to men's work."

As the captain bowed mockingly the pirate chief hailed him. "Ha, you got here quickly," he said. "No doubt to claim the wench, eh?"

Ramon nodded. "I rode two horses until they dropped," he said. "As for the girl, she is safe, though she made an attempt to escape. Fortunately your woman stopped her."

"I wish you luck with her," Bardoso said, baring his arm. "She is too much for me. She did this to my arm with a dagger, and one of my men fared as badly. You will have your hands full to tame her."

"Leave that to me," Ramon said. He motioned for Bardoso to join him where they could not be overheard.

"The governor would like this southland to be troubled as much as possible," Ramon said when the two men were out of earshot. "He would even sacrifice some of his own men if he had to."

Bardoso leaned closer. "Is there a chance of profit in what you are saying?" he whispered.

Ramon nodded. "How would you like to raid San Diego de Alcalá, with scarcely any danger?"

Bardoso's eyes grew even larger. He knew San Diego de Alcalá well. It was very rich and was home to a very wealthy mission.

Ramon knew he had snared the pirate chief in his trap. "Listen to me," he said. "You have a number of caballeros held prisoner, and the señorita also. I will go to San Diego de Alcalá and inform the *comandante* of the presidio there. He has only a few troopers under his command. As I outrank him, I will lead the troopers back here to your camp. They will think they are going to destroy your camp and rescue the prisoners. But you and your men will be ready and you can destroy them from ambush. That will leave San Diego de Alcalá open to you."

Bardoso rubbed his hands together. "By my blade, what a plan!" he said.

Ramon was quick to continue. "You must understand this must be made to look like a mistake so that no one will ever know that I or the governor had a hand in it."

"Agreed!" Bardoso said eagerly.

Ramon turned to leave. "I will speak with the señorita one more time, then I will ride like the wind to San Diego de Alcalá. You must get your men ready for the ambush. I'll return with the troopers before nightfall. You can wipe them out, sack San Diego de Alcalá, and sail down the coast of Baja California where you can establish a new camp."

Bardoso could scarcely keep from drooling at the prospect. "It shall be exactly as you say, señor. And what will be your share of the loot?"

"Nothing whatever," Captain Ramon answered, "if you keep the señorita safe for me."

"I promise her safety, Capitán!" Bardoso pledged.

Ramon smiled to himself. He left Bardoso and went to the building where the señorita was being guarded by Inez.

"You may go," he said to Inez, then turned to Lolita. "Everything is arranged," the captain whispered. "I ride for San Diego immediately. You will remain a prisoner here until I return with the troopers. Guard yourself well. We will return by nightfall, and then the pirate den will be destroyed and I will personally liberate you and the caballeros. You will then be free to return to your father."

"If you do this, I shall give you my gratitude, señor," Lolita said.

"Only your gratitude?" Ramon asked, still hoping for a change in heart from the proud girl.

"I have told you of that matter," Lolita said. "Please leave, señor!"

"I am about to risk my life to save you and your friends," Ramon said. "Am I to have no reward? One embrace?"

"Señor!"

Ramon's face reddened. "You would not speak like this if Zorro begged a kiss," he said.

"You insult me, señor," Lolita said firmly.

The captain stepped closer to Lolita who drew the rag shawl around her tightly. "One embrace is all I ask, then I shall ride. If you will not grant one, then I shall take it," he said, reaching for the girl's arm.

Lolita pulled away. "If Zorro were here you would not dare this thing," she said.

Ramon laughed aloud. "But he is not here and I am," he roared, closing the space between them.

Lolita's hand moved quickly to the handle of the dagger secreted in the folds of her shawl. But before she could draw it, something covered the window behind them, and for a moment the room was without light. "What—" cried Ramon as a figure dressed in women's clothes leaped through the window into the room. As the captain and Lolita watched in astonishment, the intruder tore off the woman's clothes that covered his own. One hand went to his sword; the other gently pushed Lolita aside. Then his head came up, and he stared boldly into the stunned eyes of Captain Ramon.

"Zorro!" Lolita cried.

Before the shocked *comandante* of the presidio of Reina de los Angeles could utter a sound, Zorro slapped his face so hard his head rocked.

Zorro had escaped from the pirate camp on the bare back of the infuriated stallion. The horse had flown so swiftly that there was no question of being overtaken, but at times the bold caballero wondered if he could make the steed stop.

Zorro guided the horse in a great circle that took him back to the pirate camp undetected. The animal paused just long enough to let him slip from its back then continued its mad race to safety.

The caballero hid above the camp where he could watch the pirates unseen. He knew he was confronted by a dire emergency. The señorita was in need of rescue, and his friends, too.

The idea to wait for nightfall before attempting a rescue left his mind as he saw Bardoso talking with none other than Captain Ramon. He hurried as quickly as he dared toward the camp, not thinking how he could enter it single-handed and undetected. His brain was filled only with the plight of the señorita and what he must do.

The smell of smoke stopped him. He peered through the brush to see a small hut with a fire smoldering in front of its door. An old woman stirred the fire once, then hobbled away toward the pirate camp below.

As soon as the woman was gone Zorro sneaked into the hut. He needed a disguise that would let him enter the pirate camp unnoticed. With one ear alert for the old woman's return, Zorro rummaged through a pile of rags. He pulled a tattered skirt and ancient shawl from among the clothes and slipped them on.

Doubling over as if he were as old as the true owner, Zorro hobbled toward the pirate camp. When he entered the camp he perceived things were calm again. The pirates were gathered around the building where the caballeros were held prisoner, and the women and children were going about their business as if nothing had disrupted their day.

Captain Ramon crossed the clearing in front of Zorro and entered a small adobe building. Zorro guessed that the little señorita was a captive inside. Slowly, so as not to call attention to himself, he circled the building and listened beneath a small window.

Ramon's voice, demanding an embrace, boomed out the open window. Zorro clenched his trusted sword hidden in the folds of the old woman's ragged shawl. He knew it would be perilous to enter the building because Ramon would summon the pirates. Unless I can silence him first, Zorro thought. But I must be quick.

Determined to spare Lolita further insults, Zorro climbed to the window just as Ramon was reaching for her.

Zorro hesitated no longer. He scrambled through the window, tearing away the woman's clothing as he hit the floor. The moment his hands were free, he drew his gleaming sword. Pushing the señorita gently to one side, he confronted his enemy.

Before the astonished pair could react, Zorro's hand cracked against Captain Ramon's head. Then he stepped back to give the renegade officer a chance to defend himself, though he little deserved it.

"You are alive!" the señorita gasped.

"Very much alive!" Zorro shouted. Then, turning to her, he said grimly, "Stand back and turn your pretty face away, for this is not going to be pleasant to watch!"

Fear creased Captain Ramon's face as he struggled to free his sword from its scabbard. "Zorro!" he cried.

"Sí! Zorro!" the caballero replied. "There is not enough water in all the sea to drown me while there remains something to be avenged. We have crossed blades before, señor, and I have marked you. But this time shall be the last, Capitán! It is an honor that I do not cut you down without giving you the chance to defend yourself!"

Captain Ramon's sword was out and he was on guard. The memory of the first time he had crossed blades with Zorro plagued him. Zorro had played with him as a cat plays with a mouse before marking him with his bold sign.

Ramon backed toward the door, knowing too well he had little chance against the sword of Zorro. Zorro blocked his escape.

"So you are a coward who would run, eh?" Zorro laughed. "A pretty soldier, that."

The terrified *comandante* began to scream at the top of his lungs. "Help me, pirates!" he shouted. "Zorro is here. Zorro has returned."

Zorro advanced but Ramon, seeing another way to save himself, grabbed Lolita and held her before him like a shield. All the while he screamed for the pirates.

"You coward!" Zorro spat. "Coward and dog!"

"Flee, Zorro!" Señorita Lolita begged. "The pirates will be here and capture you."

"Not before I have bested this arrant coward and rescued you," Zorro pledged. He advanced on

Ramon but the frightened captain backed into a corner, still holding the señorita as a shield. Zorro dared not make a move with his sword.

Inez, waiting in the other room, heard the noise and Ramon's shouts. Daring to open the door a crack, she peered in. One look told her all. Immediately, she barred the door and ran for help.

"Bardoso! Sanchez! All you devil pirates!" she cried. "Zorro is in here, and he's going to kill the captain. Come quickly and take him!"

At once Bardoso and his men ran to the building, their swords drawn. The pirates gathered inside the front room; from the storeroom came the sound of Zorro's voice.

"Hide behind a woman, eh, coward?" Zorro taunted. "Come out and fight, renegade."

In the front room Bardoso signaled to Inez to open the door. The pirate chief and his cutthroat band tumbled into the storeroom, their blades eager and ready.

"Take him alive," Bardoso thundered. "Catch me this land pirate unhurt!"

Zorro whirled to confront the pirates. His sword sang as he leaped forward to wound a man and then retreat. But the weight of numbers was against him, and in such cramped fighting quarters he could not get to the window to escape. In moments it was over. The horde of fierce pirates overwhelmed the daring caballero, and lashed his hands behind his back.

"So, Señor Zorro," Bardoso said. "We have you in our hands again. But this time it will be fire or steel, not water, that will make a real ghost of you."

Captain Ramon lurched forward, his face purple with wrath. "Do with him as you will," he said. "But let me have a hand in it."

Bardoso laughed aloud. "Ha! You had your chance, Capitán, and you did not make much of it. I'll put him in with the other caballeros." Then he turned to his men. "Take him away!"

Lolita struggled forward, but the pirates pushed her back as they took Zorro away. Only the captain remained with the small señorita.

"You must try to understand, señorita," he said. "I had to speak thus. I must keep the pirates believing I am one of them, else I cannot get to San Diego and fetch the soldiers."

Lolita glared at him. "There is no need of further pretense," she said scornfully. "I know you for what you are."

Captain Ramon laughed. "You show bravery now that you know this Señor Zorro is alive, eh?" he said. "But how long do you think he'll live in the hands of those pirates? Bardoso loves ransom money, but he'll take no ransom for Zorro. He wants vengeance."

"I cannot endure your presence any longer," Lolita said. "Leave me alone with my sorrows."

The *comandante* did not move. "Nor can I endure your scorn much longer," he said. "Has it occurred to you that you are completely in my power?"

"Your true colors show again," Lolita said.

"Do you not fear death and torture?" Captain Ramon asked. "It is what awaits this Señor Zorro, there is no doubt."

"Torture?" Lolita gasped.

"You don't think these beasts of pirates will let him die painlessly, do you?" the captain asked, sensing he was at least winning the señorita's attention, if not her allegiance. "He will beg and shriek for mercy—"

"No! No!" Lolita cried.

Ramon moved a step closer. "But yes," he said quietly. "And you will be forced to watch as they chip at him with their knives and burn his flesh—"

Lolita threw her hands to her ears. "Señor! For the love of the saints—"

"You do not like the picture, eh?" Captain Ramon said. "Wait until you see what my words cannot describe."

Lolita looked heavenward. "If only I could save him—give my life for his—" she said.

The captain spoke swiftly. "Perhaps there may be a way."

"What do you mean?" Lolita asked, clinging to his words.

Ramon looked to see that nobody was near, then said in low tones, "I can coax Bardoso to delay the torture until he has ambushed the soldiers from San Diego de Alcalá," he said. "Of course, the battle will go against him and his men as I have planned. The caballeros and Señor Zorro will be freed."

Lolita's face brightened. "And you will do this?" she asked. "Ah, señor! If only you would."

"I can—and will—for a price!" Ramon said.

Lolita drew a deep breath. "And what is the price?"

The captain put his hand on Lolita's arm. "You are the price," he said softly. "I will save Señor Zorro in return for an immediate marriage to you."

Lolita pulled away. "You beast!"

"Is it such an ill thing to wed one of His Excellency's officers?" Ramon demanded.

"I cannot do it," Lolita said. "My heart is not my own."

"How can you hesitate?" Ramon asked. "If you become my wife, Zorro will be saved from torture and death. He will be released. Without your consent, he will die."

"No!" Lolita said.

"There is little time," Ramon said. "Friar Felipe is in the camp. He can wed us—"

"I cannot," Lolita sobbed.

"Then the pirates will have their way with him," the *comandante* said.

Lolita's eyes glistened. "Is there no other way? Can't you save him without asking such a price?" she pleaded. "Can't you be a true caballero once in your life?"

"To save him and let you wed another?" Ramon's voice was cold. "It is too much to ask. The only way is for you to become my wife. I will fetch the troopers from San Diego de Alcalá, and they will vanquish the pirates. All you must do is to say I tricked the pirates, and you wed me in gratitude for saving you from them."

"Such a falsehood would not come easily from my lips," Lolita said. "And how can I trust you? How do I know you would fetch the troopers as you say?"

The captain realized he was winning. "I am not afraid to make a bargain," he said. "You need not wed me until after the pirates are defeated and the caballeros set free." Twirling his mustache, he asked, "But how may I be sure you will keep your end of the bargain once I have kept mine?"

Lolita snapped her head erect and raised her shoulders haughtily. "Señor!" she said. "Would a daughter of the Pulidos break her given word?"

A smile crossed Captain Ramon's face. "Then you give it?" he asked anxiously.

"Not yet," Lolita replied. "There are to be certain stipulations, señor."

The smile vanished as Ramon spoke. "And what are they?"

"You must allow me to see Zorro alone so I may tell him the truth about what I intend to do," Lolita said. "He must know that I will marry you only to save him and the others."

Ramon threw up his hands. "Ha!" he exclaimed. "If he knew that he would not accept the sacrifice."

"If I insist, he would," Lolita said. "Zorro would not raise a hand against you if I asked him not to do so."

The captain thought for a moment. "Perhaps it might be arranged," he said. But even as he spoke he was still scheming. He knew that once the soldiers wiped out the pirates, the señorita would keep her word. Men might despise him for taking advantage of the situation, but he would be safe. Then, for a small sum, he could have Zorro killed.

On the other hand, Ramon knew that if by some fortune of war the pirates should win, he could seize the señorita and let the pirates have Zorro. He would have to become a renegade, but the thought of becoming a pirate chief himself was not so far-fetched.

Lolita spoke, breaking Ramon's evil train of thought. "I will tell no one but Zorro," she said. "I will not betray your double-dealing to the pirates because that would mean death for the caballeros and Zorro, and much worse for me. But I must speak to Zorro before I give you a decision."

"I will arrange it with Bardoso," Ramon said eagerly. "The pirate woman will guard you until I return. But remember, you must play the game well to be successful. There is little time. I must begin my ride to San Diego de Alcalá as quickly as possible."

NINE

The Señorita's Plot

Captain Ramon found Bardoso drinking wine heavily with his men.

The pirate chief watched his approach. "Have you not started for San Diego de Alcalá yet?" he shouted drunkenly.

"Soon," Ramon answered. "But tell me, is it your intention to torture this Señor Zorro?"

Bardoso squinted his eyes into two tiny slits. "I shall make him squirm and squeal," he bellowed. "Then I shall turn him into a proper ghost."

"Death is nothing to a man like that," Ramon said quickly. "But torture, especially mental torture, is a different matter."

"Mental torture?" Bardoso said. "I do not understand."

"Torture of the mind," the captain explained. "That is the worst kind by far. If you truly wish to have some sport with Zorro, listen to me. The señorita is afraid you will torture and then kill him. I have told her I will save Zorro by fetching the troopers from San Diego de Alcalá—if she will wed me."

"This is treason," Bardoso shouted.

Ramon spoke carefully. "There is no treason between you and me, Bardoso. Listen. She will tell

Zorro my plan, that she will wed me to save him. Imagine the torture he will suffer when he hears that and is unable to prevent it."

Bardoso began to smile as he listened. "But why work so hard to get a wench to agree to marry you when you can take her at your pleasure?" he asked, still unsure of the captain's plan.

Ramon was ready. "Because it will destroy Zorro," he said. "When I return with the soldiers, you can overpower them and then loot San Diego de Alcalá. Later you can do with Zorro as you wish in celebration of your victory."

Bardoso slapped Ramon on the back. "Spoken like one of us," he said.

"There is more," Ramon said. "If you truly want to torture him, keep him to the last. Kill the other caballeros first and force Zorro to watch. That will hurt more than torture itself."

Bardoso roared with glee. "You should have been born a pirate."

"Then it is agreed?" Ramon asked quickly.

"Sí!" Bardoso shouted. "It is agreed."

Ramon turned to the building where Lolita waited. "Then I shall take the señorita to Zorro now."

Bardoso stayed his arm. "There are two rooms in the building where Zorro is held captive. Zorro is alone in the front room. I thought it best to keep him separate from the other caballeros. The señorita can visit him in the front room, and we will be at the window, listening to his agony as she tells him her fate."

Captain Ramon hastened back to Lolita and told her he had arranged things as she wished. Then, he escorted her to the adobe building where Zorro and the caballeros were being held prisoners. As

Señorita Lolita went inside Bardoso and his men gathered outside the window.

The señorita stepped forward slowly, a look of anguish in her eyes. Zorro smiled down at her.

"The saints are good, señorita, that I may see you again," he whispered.

Lolita interrupted him, "It is a sad errand that brings me here, Zorro."

Zorro's face turned grim. "They have sent you to tell me I am to die, is that it? I do not fear death, for it is but another adventure. It is for you that I fear."

"Fear not for me nor death," Lolita said. "I have come to tell you you are to go free."

Zorro stepped back. "Free?" he said. "Has Friar Felipe shown these devil pirates the error of their ways that they are now honest men who will free me? Or have you only tried to soften my true sentence? Speak!"

Lolita turned her face down, unable to look into Zorro's eyes. "Captain Ramon has arranged for you to go free."

"Do not trust Ramon," Zorro said.

Lolita continued. "He told me he is tricking the pirates. He is to ride to San Diego de Alcalá and return with the troopers. They will vanquish the pirates, and you and the caballeros will be saved."

Zorro was truly puzzled. "Ramon would do this?" he said. "Is there a hidden streak of goodness in the beast?"

Lolita lifted her eyes and looked forlornly into Zorro's face. "He will do it for a price."

Zorro slapped his knee. "I should have known. Well, I can pay the dog. Tell me how much he wants."

"It is not money he wants," Lolita said with a sigh. "The price is that I wed him."

Zorro reeled backward as if struck by a blow. "You? Wed a snake like Captain Ramon?"

Lolita put out her hand. "Only to save you," she said. "But he asks my word, the word of a Pulido. In return the wedding is not to take place until he returns with the troopers, the pirates are slain, and you are free."

Zorro shook his head. "I cannot allow it," he said.

"Unless you do, you will face torture and death," Lolita said. "But I shall remain true to my heart. After the ceremony, before he can claim me, I shall die—"

"And do you think I would accept such a sacrifice?" Zorro demanded. "Could I live to see you give your life for mine? Never, señorita, never!"

Lolita was near tears. "If I do not marry him, they will torture you to death."

"So be it," Zorro said. "You cannot do this thing. You are a Pulido. I entreat you—"

"If I refuse, we will both die," Lolita said.

"Better to die defending your honor than to have your name linked with his, even for a moment. You must give up this plan. All hope is not gone. They have taken my sword and my hands are bound, but the spirit of Zorro still burns in my breast. Given a little time, I'll win through."

With that spark of hope, Lolita changed her tone to a whisper. "Perhaps I can hold him off for an hour," she said. "I have just thought of something."

"What is it?" Zorro asked quietly so no one could hear.

"Pretend that you agree to do as I asked," Lolita said softly. "Let me embrace you. They are listening and may be watching so keep your back away from that window."

Bardoso and Captain Ramon were watching. They saw Lolita embrace Zorro, but Zorro's back was turned from them and they could not see what she was doing.

As Lolita embraced Zorro she slipped the small dagger from her shawl and began to saw away the ropes binding his wrists. "Be careful," she said when the ropes were split. "Do not let them see what I have done."

Zorro put his mouth close to the little señorita's ear. "Never was there a señorita like you," he whispered. "Once again I have hope."

"Don't let them see it in your face," Lolita cautioned. She took her arms from around Zorro, but as she did she slipped the dagger into the sash at his waist. Only then did she raise her voice.

"It is the only way, Zorro," she said convincingly. "I must give my word to Captain Ramon." She turned away from him quickly, and ran to the door.

Ramon was waiting outside for her. "You have decided?" he said.

Lolita looked imploringly into the captain's face. "I am nearly ready to give my word," she said. "But first I must have an hour with Friar Felipe so that he may pray with me."

"I'm growing tired of waiting," Ramon grumbled. "I should be on my way already. Why can't you decide now?"

"There will be ample time to return with the troopers before nightfall," Lolita said. "Give me only an hour."

"Very well," Captain Ramon said. "An hour. I will send for the friar. You will both be under guard in a hut until you make up your mind."

Zorro fought to keep the joy from showing on his face as Lolita left. She had cut his bonds and given him a weapon. The rest would be up to him, and he was confident he would prevail over his enemies.

Zorro peered out the window and across the clearing. Nearby was the hut where the caballeros' weapons, including Zorro's own beloved sword, were locked and guarded. As he studied the hut, Sanchez rode wildly into the clearing on a magnificent horse. It was Toranado, Zorro's own prized stallion.

"The foul pirate found Toranado where I left him on the night I followed that dark-hearted band to their ship," he said to himself.

Sanchez left the horse near the hut as he hurried off in search of Bardoso; and Zorro hurried to the door between his cell and the room where the other caballeros were being held.

"Audre," he whispered when he was sure no guard would overhear him. "I have another chance. My hands are free. I have a small weapon, and Toranado is here just outside my window. We are outnumbered by the pirates, but if I escape to San Diego de Alcalá, I can return with the troopers."

"Then you must leave at once," Don Audre said through the heavy door.

"Whatever happens here, you must look after the señorita," Zorro said.

"Be assured of that," his friend replied. "The saints be with you."

Zorro returned to the window. Outside, Toranado pawed the ground impatiently. A few guards were around, but their attention strayed as they talked, drank, gambled, and argued among themselves.

Zorro desired his own sword, but knew the risk getting it would be too great. The pirates would cut him down before he got across the clearing. He decided it would be far better to seize the horse and ride at top speed to San Diego de Alcalá for help. There would be time to settle scores when he returned.

He returned to the door and called to his friend again. "Don Audre? You must help me by making a commotion. Pretend you are fighting among yourselves. The diversion will hold the guards' attention while I do my best to escape."

In moments a fearsome din arose from the room filled with caballeros. They shrieked and shouted and pounded on the door as if a terrible fight were underway.

Zorro ran to the window and shouted to the guards. "Come quickly," he called. "My friends are fighting among themselves. You must stop them!"

But the guards didn't budge. "So what if they kill each other?" one laughed. "It will save us the work."

But Bardoso heard the commotion and raced to the hut, screaming for the guards to follow him. "If they destroy themselves we will collect no ransom," he bellowed. "Unfasten the door. But don't let them escape."

Bardoso entered Zorro's room with the guards. Although the pirate chief gave Zorro a glance, his attention was on the door leading to the room filled with screaming caballeros. The guards also paid little heed to Zorro whose hands were still bound behind his back—or so they thought.

The moment the door to the caballeros' room was thrown open, Zorro ran for the door leading outside. He dispatched two guards quickly, and dashed into the clearing where Toranado stood. Zorro shot a quick glance around the camp, hoping he might spy the señorita whom he would then take with him, but she was not in sight.

With his dagger clenched tightly between his teeth, Zorro leaped atop the huge horse's back. As guards poured from the hut after him he jabbed his spurs into the horse's flanks, and Toranado burst into a full gallop.

A pistol barked and its ball whistled perilously close to Zorro's head, but he was free. He bent low over Toranado's neck and rode wildly across the clearing and up the slope. Another pistol ball scored the air, but it too flew by. Once he was over the crest he would be safe. The pirates would not dare follow him to San Diego de Alcalá.

However, there was one more obstacle. As the madly galloping horse neared the edge of the clearing, Captain Ramon jumped in front of it, his sword drawn. Must I match his sword with this small dagger? Zorro thought. But Ramon did not dare stand up to the charging animal. He leaped out of its path, and Toranado raced up the slope with Zorro riding proudly in the saddle, singing at the top of his voice:

"*Atención!* A caballero's near—" It was his way of letting the little señorita know he was free and already on his way for help.

As Captain Ramon watched Zorro race up the slope to safety, he saw his own future hanging by a very thin thread. He sensed Zorro was on his way to the presidio at San Diego de Alcalá for help. And he knew he must get there first, with a far better story to tell.

The dishonored captain ran toward the hut where Bardoso stood cursing Zorro's escape. "What happened?" Ramon shouted.

Bardoso was furious. "He tricked us!" the pirate chief shouted. "If that wench had anything to do with it—"

"The girl is not to be harmed," Captain Ramon said firmly. "Zorro is riding for San Diego de Alcalá for help, I am certain. I must beat him there. The lieutenant will take orders from me, and I will return with the troopers and you can ambush them as we originally planned. Now get me a horse!"

"And what of this Señor Zorro?" Bardoso asked.

"I will have him imprisoned at the presidio," Ramon said. "After you defeat the soldiers and loot the town, he will be at your mercy."

Bardoso rubbed his thick black beard. "You think of everything," he said. "I still say you should be a pirate."

A fine horse was produced by one of Bardoso's men. The captain sprang into the saddle. "Arrange the ambush at the head of the canyon, as we planned," Captain Ramon said. "Don't delay. I'll lead the soldiers straight into the trap." Then he spurred his mount and dashed up the slope in the wake of the fleeing Zorro.

Ramon knew the country thoroughly, and rode an excellent horse. More important, he knew a shortcut to San Diego, which he was certain Zorro did not. Stopping at the crest of the hill for a moment, he listened. The distant thunder of Toranado's hoofbeats proved he was right—Zorro was taking the long way. Ramon would reach San Diego long before the caballero. He turned his mount toward the shortcut and spurred him on.

As the black-hearted captain rode toward San Diego de Alcalá he reviewed his treacherous plan. Once there he would have Zorro thrown into the guardroom at the presidio. Then, leading the troopers, he would return to the pirate camp. Though Bardoso would be expecting to ambush the troopers, Ramon would instead surprise the pirates and wipe them out. After that he would release the caballeros and the señorita, persuading everyone he had been continuously true and loyal.

There was more. He would then convince the authorities that Zorro was an ally of the pirates and have him hanged. He would ask his friend the governor to order the señorita to wed him as a prize for saving her and wiping out the pirate brood. The señorita would have to obey the governor. And Captain Ramon would then have everything he ever wanted.

The possibility the pirates might win against the soldiers did not escape the captain's dark plans. In that event he would continue to pretend to side with the pirates and become one of them. He would still get the señorita.

The captain rode fiercely along the trail, determined to reach San Diego de Alcalá before Zorro. At last he reached the outskirts of the settlement. Inquisitive heads poked out from huts along the way, and children and chickens leaped to avoid being run down by the flying horse. On top of a hill ahead of him was the presidio. In minutes he was there.

Captain Ramon dismounted in a crowd of troopers who gathered to see what the excitement was. Ramon ignored their salutes, heading straight for the *comandante*'s office.

Ramon had lied nobly to Bardoso. He had told the pirate there were only a few troopers at the presidio. Instead there was an extra contingent, many more than usual, and their *comandante*, a mere lieutenant, would have to take orders from the captain.

The lieutenant sprang to his feet the moment Captain Ramon entered his office.

Ramon wasted no time with civil talk. "Order your trumpeter to sound assembly," he said flatly. "This is a serious matter—and urgent!"

The lieutenant, a good soldier, did not question his superior but immediately ordered the trumpeter to call the men together.

"There is a large pirate camp within eight miles of here," Ramon went on. "Three nights ago they raided Reina de los Angeles."

The junior officer nodded. "Yes, we heard of their raid."

Captain Ramon continued. "I followed them by land. Early this morning I found their camp. They have taken prisoner some caballeros who pursued them. And the señorita Lolita Pulido is a prisoner as well."

"Where is the camp?" the lieutenant asked.

"A few miles up the coast," Ramon answered. "You should be warned—Señor Zorro is mixed up with them. His wild blood has broken out again. The señorita thinks he was trying to rescue her. The truth is he had her stolen to satisfy his lawlessness. Once he is captured, it will be the end of this menace."

The lieutenant's eyes were fixed on Ramon; he was completely taken in by the lies.

"One more thing," Ramon said, determined to seal Zorro's fate. "I overheard a plot in the making. Zorro himself will ride here. He will tell you the caballeros and the señorita are prisoners so he can lure you and your men into a pirate ambush. Once the troopers are out of the way, he and the pirates will be free to loot San Diego de Alcalá. Nobody will be left to stop them."

"The fiend!" the lieutenant gasped. "How can I help you?"

Ramon smiled. His plan was working perfectly. "Have a half dozen of your men here and ready when he arrives. Once he begins his story, have him seized. Throw him into the guardroom in a strait-jacket. I'll help you lead your troop against the pirates. We'll attack from the rear where they don't expect us. We will rescue the caballeros and the señorita, and you will be a hero. A promotion is guaranteed."

The lieutenant's eager face beamed. "It is agreed!"

"Be quick," Captain Ramon said. "There is little time. Once Zorro is captured and word of his deceit is out, he'll be punished by hanging and that will be the end of him."

The lieutenant leaped from his chair to carry out Ramon's grim plan just as the office door flew open and Zorro burst into the room.

TEN

A Double-cross

Zorro was dumbfounded to see Captain Ramon in the lieutenant's office at the presidio of San Diego de Alcalá. The scheming officer was the last person he'd seen at the pirate's camp, and even though Zorro had ridden at great speed, here he was facing him once again.

Zorro realized instantly the captain had taken a shortcut. He also knew he was in grave danger. His hand went to his small dagger, a paltry weapon but the only one he had. The two officers already had their swords drawn.

"So, you got here ahead of me, did you, you renegade traitor?" Zorro said to Captain Ramon.

"'Tis you who are the renegade traitor and friend of pirates," the captain cried.

Zorro began to suspect the treachery. "So that is the tale you have told," he said. He turned to the lieutenant. "I am Zorro," he said. "Perhaps you have heard of me?"

Before the stunned lieutenant could reply, Captain Ramon spoke. "I am sure the lieutenant knows of Señor Zorro, the outlaw!"

Zorro continued to address the lieutenant. "There is a pirate camp a few miles from here," he said. "I have just escaped from it to tell you there is a señorita and several caballeros held prisoner there who must be rescued before they are tortured."

Ramon stepped between Zorro and the lieutenant. "Escape?" he exclaimed. "You did not escape. You came here to lead the lieutenant's troopers into a trap. Luckily the lieutenant is already planning to ride to the rescue. But you will remain his prisoner here, tied in a straitjacket."

Zorro was amazed at the captain's cleverness. "Make no mistake about it, Lieutenant," he said. "Even though Captain Ramon outranks you, he is the traitor. He is in league with the pirates himself."

The lieutenant had regained his composure. He laughed as he asked, "You scarcely expect me to believe that?"

Zorro was astounded. "You believe Captain Ramon over me?"

The lieutenant nodded. "I do," he said curtly. "Señor Zorro, until the rescue is accomplished, you will be held here. There will be an investigation of this whole affair."

Zorro's eyes narrowed. "It will not be necessary to keep me a prisoner," he said. "Lead your soldiers as you will, but be quick about it. Do not listen to Captain Ramon. The señorita held captive is Lolita Pulido, who I have sworn to protect. Allow me to remain free to aid in her rescue."

The lieutenant shook his head. "I am sorry," he said. "Captain Ramon has preferred a charge against you. You must remain a prisoner at the presidio."

The lieutenant placed a whistle to his lips that would summon guards, but Zorro, who had no intention of being kept prisoner, knocked it to the floor.

At once the lieutenant drew his sword on Zorro who was armed only with the small dagger. Though the officer's weapon was much larger, Zorro's skill was greater. As the officer lunged, Zorro leaped aside, warding off the blow. But the move allowed Captain Ramon to reach the door where he shouted for guards. Then the captain, his own sword pointed at Zorro's throat, joined the fray.

Zorro realized he couldn't hold off two men with only a small blade. He fought well and skillfully, but they closed in on him, one on either side.

As the lieutenant made another inexperienced leap for Zorro, the caballero dropped to his knees. With a nearby chair, he tripped the young officer who toppled to the floor.

Zorro leaped to his feet as Ramon, his sword slashing madly, advanced. At the moment the captain's sword arm was stretched out full length, Zorro pitched his tiny dagger with superb skill. The blade pierced the officer's uniform coat and stuck sharply in the wall, pinning Ramon for the precious moments Zorro needed to flee.

Zorro raced for the office window and leaped out just as the guards rushed in the opposite door. The bold caballero landed on his feet and ran to where he had left Toranado.

Bad luck turned to disaster. The horse was gone. In its place was the full troop of soldiers mounted in their own saddles. Zorro turned to flee but the men on horseback quickly surrounded him. Heeding the lieutenant's shouts to capture Zorro, the circle of mounted soldiers closed in.

Seeing his slim hopes fading, Zorro scurried beneath the belly of the nearest horse, breaking safely out of the ring of stunned soldiers.

Zorro ran to a low building and scampered up the wall using the rough masonry as if it were a ladder. He darted across the building's roof and slid down the tiles on the opposite side, stopping just before reaching the edge. A glance below told him his horse was there, being groomed by a young hostler. The caballero didn't hesitate. Springing from a crouch he flew off the roof and into Toranado's saddle. The youth fell to the ground as the horse bolted, but Zorro held on.

Quickly, Zorro turned the beast's head toward the highway, his only route of escape. He urged the horse with his heels, but the noble beast was exhausted from the earlier ride and was no match for the troopers' fresh mounts. They surrounded him in moments.

Unarmed, Zorro was helpless. The soldiers pulled him from his saddle and marched him back to the lieutenant's office where the two officers were waiting.

"A straitjacket for him," the lieutenant commanded. "And then into the guardroom. Two men will remain behind to see he does not escape, though I scarcely think even Señor Zorro can escape a straitjacket."

"You are making a sad mistake," Zorro said. "I tell you it is Captain Ramon who is the traitor. Don't listen to him. Ride swiftly and free the prisoners. Take the señorita to a safe place. But I ask again, let me ride with you."

"I have given my orders," the lieutenant said.

Zorro struggled in the soldiers' grasp, but there were ten of them and only one of him. "I swear by my honor as a caballero that I have told you the truth, Lieutenant," he shouted. "Does that mean nothing to you?"

The lieutenant hesitated. Honor was something an officer understood well. But that was precisely why he could not believe Captain Ramon was disloyal.

Ramon stepped forward, unwilling to take the chance that Zorro's plea might sway the young officer's mind. "It is true that for a caballero to swear by his honor is a sacred thing," he said. "But all the more reason to despise one who would use that honor lightly as Señor Zorro has by falsely charging me."

The lieutenant hesitated for a moment then faced the caballero. "I have decided," he said. "You will be held in a straitjacket until we return." He turned to his soldiers and gave the command.

Zorro tried to fight but it was useless. Struggling wildly, he was taken to the guardroom, where the soldiers lashed his feet and wrists together and then bound him in a leather straitjacket. The soldiers ignored his loud protests. They propped him up on a bench and left. There was the sound of the guardroom door being barred, and then the room became silent.

Zorro sat helplessly as the sound of horses' hooves faded in the distance. Captain Ramon and the troop were on the way to the pirate camp while he remained behind, as helpless as a worm in a cocoon.

Bardoso had turned mean. Zorro's dramatic escape following the fight between the pirates and the caballeros inflamed his anger like oil poured on hot coals. He faced the building where the caballeros were held prisoner, his feet wide apart, his tiny eyes glaring ominously.

Sanchez and the other pirates knew to keep out of their chief's way when he was like this. When Bardoso bellowed for his lieutenant, Sanchez approached warily.

"Sanchez!" Bardoso bellowed. "We have grown soft because we lack proper sport. Since we have prisoners, what say you to a little torture? Burning one of those high-born caballeros at the stake would remind a pirate of his calling."

"But there is an ambush to be prepared for," Sanchez said.

"There is time for that," Bardoso answered. "We can fight better if we have more wine to drink and some sport to inspire us before giving battle."

"And which caballero shall be roasted?" Sanchez asked. "They are all valuable for ransom."

"One can be spared," Bardoso said. "We'll just ask more ransom for the others." He started for the adobe building housing the prisoners. "Come. We'll force them to gamble to decide which among them will be the victim."

Followed by Sanchez and a half dozen trusted men, Bardoso unfastened the outer door and entered with his men at his heels. They waited as he unlocked the inner door and threw it open.

The caballeros were sprawled around the room talking in low tones. Their faces were full of scorn for the pirate chief who walked among them.

"So you raised a din to distract us while Señor Zorro escaped, eh?" Bardoso said. "It is in my mind there must be some punishment for that."

Bardoso extended his hand. In it was a deck of cards. He put the deck on a bench, face down. "You will form a line and walk past this bench," he said. "Each man will draw a card. The first to draw a deuce will be the victim."

The caballeros stirred. They knew pirate ways and what being the victim meant.

Don Audre Ruiz stepped from among the caballeros. "And suppose we do not care to play your game?" he said sarcastically.

Bardoso glared at the caballero. "The solution to that is easy," he said. "Since you are their leader here, we'll roast you first, and two others picked at random as well."

Don Audre stood his ground. "Your punishment will be swift if you do this thing," he said.

"Ha!" Bardoso roared. "But you will not be here to see it if you are roasted first." Then to the caballeros he snapped, "Line up, prisoners, and let me see you tremble."

Don Audre put his face in Bardoso's. "Caballeros do not know the existence of fear," he sneered. "But if you have the courage and spirit of fair play, let me fight it out with any two of your fiendish crew, a dagger against long blades."

Bardoso laughed aloud. "Do I look the fool?" he shouted. "Why run a needless chance when we have you powerless already? Now line up and choose cards."

The caballeros formed a line with Sergeant Garcia at the very end. One by one they drew cards from the greasy pack. No one drew a dreaded deuce.

"Fortunate caballeros," Bardoso said. "But a deuce will appear soon, and we shall have our sport—" He stopped abruptly as Don Audre turned over his card. It was the deuce of spades!

"Indeed!" Bardoso shrieked. "How appropriate! As their leader you can show them how to die."

Don Audre flicked the card to the floor and wiped his hands as if the grim bit of pasteboard had soiled them. He looked Bardoso straight in the eyes.

"How soon?" he asked, with no emotion in his voice.

Bardoso slapped his knee. "Why, right now," he chuckled. "My men crave sport. And while you shriek for mercy, they can drink the wine we took from Reina de los Angeles."

Don Audre held himself proudly. "Are you human enough to let me speak with Friar Felipe before I die?"

"I will see that he is at the stake so you can pray with him through the smoke," Bardoso laughed.

There was a sudden jostling in the crowd of caballeros as Sergeant Garcia shouldered his way to the front.

"Foul pirate!" he cried. "Let us make a deal. I am a bigger man than this caballero and will roast better. Also I wear the uniform of the governor, whom you hate. And I'm a coward and will squirm where he will not."

"You want to die in his place?" Bardoso asked.

"I did not get a chance to draw a card," the sergeant said. "My luck would have me draw a deuce."

Don Audre put his hand on the sergeant's arm. "This is useless, my friend," he said.

"Not so!" Sergeant Garcia said. "You are a fine gentleman, a caballero, and amount to something in this world. I am just a poor soldier. Many better men can fill my place."

Don Audre smiled at the big sergeant. "Whatever your station in life, you are now a caballero and a very brave man."

Bardoso was laughing aloud at the exchange. "A hero," he scoffed. "And a fool. But I cannot let you take the caballero's place. However, since you wish to be roasted, I grant the wish. Nothing will be lost since nobody in the world would ransom you for as much as a bottle of thin wine."

"You are wrong, Bardoso," Don Audre Ruiz said. Then, turning to his men he addressed them with conviction. "Friends, promise me this last request— have your people make up a purse to ransom this soldier. He has been a friend of Zorro for years, and now I understand why. He is a man of substance."

The caballeros surged toward the pirates, but they were unarmed and the pirates' blades held them back.

Bardoso was impatient. "Come, señor," he said to Don Audre. "It is not polite for a gentlemen to keep my men waiting for their fun."

Don Audre walked among his men shaking their hands in farewell. Then the pirates bound his hands and led him from the room.

The clearing outside the building filled with shouting pirates, women, and children who came running at the news of what was to occur. A stake was made ready and Don Audre Ruiz was lashed to it amid the shrieks and insults of the pirate camp. The pirates danced like savages around the stake while women and children hurled stones at the helpless caballero.

"We'll see in a few minutes if you will squirm or not," Bardoso said to Don Audre.

"You promised me I could speak with the friar," the caballero said calmly. "But I did not think a pirate could keep his given word."

Bardoso stood back as if offended. "Ha!" he laughed. "I'll show you that I can play at having gentle blood. A matter of honor, is it?" He turned to his men. "Fetch me the fat friar at once."

As the dancing, drinking and shouting continued, fuel was heaped on the pyre at Don Audre's feet. Bardoso, his arms folded across his chest, waited to give the word to a man holding a flaming torch to light it. As all waited, the friar appeared from the crowd.

"What is this grim business you would have me do?" he asked.

"We intend to broil this caballero," Bardoso said. "But first he needs a priest, so we sent for you."

Friar Felipe understood the desperate situation immediately. Normally Bardoso was very superstitious in matters concerning men of the church. But with the false courage of wine in him, the friar knew an appeal to the pirate chief would be useless.

To the surprise of all, the friar threw back his head and laughed aloud. Even Bardoso was startled.

"I thought you were a true pirate leader," the friar said so all could hear. "But you have been duped."

Bardoso put his nose to the friar's. "How is this?" he roared.

"You are an utter and simple fool," the friar continued. "You have placed your trust in Captain Ramon who is at this very moment riding back from San Diego de Alcalá I am sure, with troopers enough to destroy you."

Bardoso laughed aloud so that his huge chest quaked.

"Ha!" he roared. "I know that. He is leading the troopers into my ambush."

The friar shook his head slowly. "You are such an easy dupe," he said. "The señorita has told me his real plans. While you form your ambush at the head of the canyon, he'll attack from the rear and annihilate you. He will win favor with decent men and the governor, and will claim the señorita as his prize. Señor Pirate, you must know that a man who can be a traitor to one cause can be traitor to another."

Bardoso's face grew bright red. "Lies!" he roared.

"They are not lies," Friar Felipe said calmly. "And you are playing games here while you should be preparing for battle. Oh, you will be easy victims for the troopers."

Bardoso's rage cooled. There was a quality in the friar's speech that suggested he was telling the truth.

Suddenly Inez thrust herself before Bardoso. "He speaks the truth," she cried. "I overheard the *comandante* tell the señorita he was tricking you. Captain Ramon is a double traitor! Don't be caught in his trap. The man at the stake can wait. Let him meditate on his fate while you make ready to fight the soldiers."

"By my naked blade," Bardoso said. "Catch me in a trap, eh? I'll prepare a trap for him, and not in the canyon."

The pirate chief rushed off shouting orders as Friar Felipe spoke to Don Audre Ruiz, still bound at the stake.

"I had to save your life, caballero," the friar said.

"Cut me loose," Don Audre said.

The friar studied the caballero's bonds. A chain glistened among the ropes and thongs.

"There is a chain," the friar said. "I'll find a tool."

The burly friar shuffled away quickly. Don Audre Ruiz remained lashed to the stake.

At the presidio of San Diego de Alcalá, Zorro wondered if his usual good fortune had abandoned him. His case seemed hopeless. He was a prisoner.

Captain Ramon was leading the troopers against the pirates. And his beloved señorita and the caballeros were in grave peril.

But there were things happening that Zorro could not know about. Bernardo, the man who had saved Zorro and guided him to the pirate camp, had gone to San Diego de Alcalá to visit friends while he waited for news of the fight. He had been near the presidio when Captain Ramon arrived, and had watched in secret as Zorro galloped up a short while later. He had seen Zorro's attempt to escape just as he had witnessed Captain Ramon's departure with the troopers. He knew Zorro was a prisoner in the presidio, bound inside a straitjacket.

Bernardo remembered how Zorro had fought for the people when they were being persecuted by the governor, and he decided he would repay the brave caballero for his good deeds.

At the hut of a cousin Bernardo borrowed a bottle of potent palm wine—a drink everyone knew could make a man insane. He spilled some of the wine on his ragged clothes and put some on his tongue to flavor his breath. Then he approached the presidio.

The guards outside Zorro's prison hut watched as Bernardo staggered toward them waving the bottle of wine. One grabbed him by the arm.

"Don't you know it is forbidden by the governor for natives to drink this stuff?" the soldier barked.

Although Bernardo could hear, he played the part of a complete mute, waving the bottle in a defiant gesture that the guards did not take lightly.

The second soldier joined the first. "What's this?" he said. "You dare to mock the governor's soldiers?"

Bernardo again wagged the bottle in an insulting way. To ensure the soldiers' wrath he flung some wine at them.

"You are tempting fate," the first soldier said.

Bernardo looked at the soldiers with a crooked smile and threw out his chest as if to invite imprisonment.

The soldiers, who could take no more of the goading, cuffed Bernardo soundly. To their surprise, he fought back.

"Into the guardroom you go," the first soldier said. "The *comandante* will deal with you when he gets back."

The soldiers grabbed the bottle of palm wine and threw the fisherman into the guardroom. "That will teach you to defy his excellency," the second soldier said.

The soldiers barred the door but remained to peer in through the small window. Bernardo picked himself off the floor and staggered around as if drunk. He stopped as if frozen when he saw Zorro, bound in the straitjacket in the corner. Then to the soldiers' surprise he seemed offended to find himself in the same cell with an outlaw. Avoiding Zorro, he threw out his chest proudly and strutted around the room like a peacock.

The two soldiers stood laughing at the fisherman's antics. Suddenly the man fell to the floor in a stupor and a moment later began to snore loudly.

"This is powerful wine," the first soldier said, holding the half-empty bottle.

"Perhaps we should try a little," the second said.

Zorro had said nothing through all of this. He had, of course, recognized Bernardo at once.

Bernardo opened an eye and winked.

"They are drinking the wine," Zorro said quietly.

Bernardo rose to his feet. He held up a finger to signal Zorro to wait until the soldiers had drunk more wine. Both men listened as the sounds of the soldiers' footsteps faded.

Bernardo moved cautiously along the wall until he was next to Zorro. From beneath his tattered shirt, he drew a short, razor-edged fishing knife.

"I will make you rich for this," Zorro said.

Bernardo shook his head. He put his hand to his heart and then touched Zorro's chest, swearing a silent allegiance to the masked caballero who had done so much for the people.

Zorro nodded in complete understanding.

Bernardo went swiftly to work with his blade. With practiced strokes he sliced the leather strait-jacket. In moments it lay in tatters on the floor.

"We must both escape," Zorro said.

Bernardo gestured to the window and made a sign with his hands that told Zorro of a horse nearby. Another motion described daggers on the wall outside their small cell.

Zorro flexed his stiff limbs to return their circula-tion. He was ready to act. "Pound on the door as if you are fighting for your life," he instructed.

Thunder rolled from the door as Bernardo kicked it silly. Instantly the sound of footsteps warned that the guards were coming back. The soldiers peered into the room through the small window in the door. They could see neither prisoner, but the tat-tered straitjacket lying on the floor was in clear view. They opened the door and rushed in.

Zorro leaped on the first one as he entered, roll-ing him across the room. He whirled as the second man attacked, and a solid blow of his fist knocked the soldier unconscious. The first soldier jumped to his feet.

Zorro had no quarrel with the men and did not wish to harm them, but he had to prevent them pursuing him. He braced himself and ran past the man, followed closely by Bernardo. They were outside the door before the soldiers realized what was happening.

Zorro shot the door bolt home, locking the men in their own guardhouse.

"*Adios*, señors," he laughed. He turned to Bernardo. "We make our escape to safety, and to settle a score with Captain Ramon!"

Bernardo waved as the caballero leaped onto Toranado's broad back. "Await my return at Reina de los Angeles," Zorro shouted.

Bernardo smiled. He would serve Zorro with his life to the end of his days.

ELEVEN

✺

Justice Is Served

Riding with the lieutenant at the head of the column of troopers, Captain Ramon considered his plans.

He had told Bardoso to arrange to ambush the soldiers at the head of the canyon while his real intent was to attack from the rear with those same soldiers, cutting the pirates off from their camp. He had no doubt of the outcome. Though the pirates and soldiers were equal in number, the soldiers were seasoned troops and would know how to handle themselves in battle. Also, the troopers carried loaded pistols. The pirates had no ammunition for theirs. To decide the matter, the troopers would use swords against the heavy cutlasses.

Captain Ramon realized that once Bardoso discovered his treachery he could no longer return to his side. But certain that the soldiers would win, he felt secure enough to fight with them as a loyal officer.

The troopers rode swiftly along the dusty highway, wanting to complete their work before nightfall.

As the soldiers approached the canyon mouth, Ramon searched for signs of the pirates. Seeing none, he presumed they were in hiding, waiting for the troopers to ride into their ambush.

Just before his men were about to ride into the canyon and Bardoso's ambush, Ramon shouted an order and the troop galloped up the slope toward the pirate camp. Captain Ramon chuckled as he thought of Bardoso's outrage when the pirate realized he had been double-crossed.

The soldiers reached the crest overlooking the pirate camp. There was very little activity in the camp and no sign of the pirates.

"They are at the end of the canyon wondering why we didn't enter," Ramon boasted. "Now ride to them at a gallop from this end of the canyon and they will be at our mercy. Forward!"

The troopers swept down the slope, back toward the canyon's mouth, where Captain Ramon was certain the confused pirates waited. But Ramon was wrong. The sound of firearms and whistling bullets met his ears as Bardoso's men poured from the pirate huts screeching battle cries, eager to wipe out the soldiers who had tricked them.

The two sides came together, the pirates fighting like madmen to save themselves from the hangman's noose that awaited them if they were captured, and the soldiers fighting to do just that.

Bardoso spotted Ramon. "Traitor!" he screamed.

Captain Ramon did not advance with his men but kept to the rear. His sword was the only blade not reddened in the pitch of battle.

The captain had no intention of liberating the caballeros until the fight was over; he wanted to claim full credit for their rescue. He also wanted to talk to Señorita Lolita before her friends reached her. She had not made the promise she said she would, and now that Zorro was no longer a prisoner at the pirate camp, it was not necessary. But the devious captain hoped to extract a promise from the young girl yet, and secure an immediate marriage by claiming he was the only man who could give testimony to save Zorro if he was tried for conspiracy against the governor.

The battle raged on. The pirates remained between the troopers and the building where the caballeros were held prisoners. Friar Felipe had been unable to return to Don Audre before the fighting began, and the caballero remained bound to the stake.

The señorita was under the close guard of a single pirate appointed by Bardoso himself. She was in one of the adobe buildings, but Captain Ramon did not know which one.

The battle wore on with men fighting hand to hand, up and down the camp and along the sandy beach.

"Set fire to the huts," Ramon ordered. "We'll burn them out."

Within moments the camp was in flames as the dry huts crackled and burned, fed by the palm fronds that roofed them. But the battle remained an even one, and Captain Ramon was worried. It became clear that to win he would have to set the caballeros free to join the soldiers.

Smoke and flaming debris flew into the air and drifted across the sky as the battle continued. The pirates were now driving the soldiers back.

As Don Audre Ruiz watched the fight in helpless fascination from his place at the stake, a shiver of stark terror passed through him at an even greater helplessness. A flaming ember the size of a man's fist plummeted from the smoky sky and landed on the dry wood stacked around his feet. The first crackle told him the pyre was lit. His fate was sealed, not by human hands, but by the winds of chance.

Raw red flames leaped from the ring of fuel surrounding him and clawed at his clothes only minutes away from claiming him. Don Audre Ruiz was doomed.

Zorro thanked the saints that Toranado was an animal of such endurance and speed. He kicked at the horse's firm flanks and rode like the wind toward the pirate camp. He knew he would not reach the camp before Captain Ramon and the soldiers.

The sound of battle caused the caballero to rein his mount for a moment. He rode to the edge of a crest. Below, amid the smoke and flames of the burning camp, the fight raged on.

It was an even fight, neither side gaining nor losing ground. There was no sign of the caballeros. Zorro realized they were still prisoners. He kicked Toranado's flanks and rode headlong down the slope. Galloping fiercely among the burning huts, he raced to the building where the caballeros were being held.

Zorro sprang from his horse and dashed into the building. With a single blow of a metal bar he smashed the lock. The caballeros were free!

"Follow me to your weapons!" he shouted. "Fight with the troopers against the pirates. But remember, Ramon is mine!"

The caballeros answered with glad shouts, rushing to where their captured weapons were kept. The hut's roof was already ablaze. Zorro kicked in the door, leaped inside, and began tossing out swords. As the caballeros rushed forward to claim their weapons Zorro found his own beloved blade. Now armed, the caballeros ran to the fight.

Sergeant Garcia ran behind Zorro. "Zorro," he shouted. "What is this talk of my captain being a traitor?"

"It is true," Zorro called back. "He is a double traitor. He was in league with the pirates but now has turned against them. Now after them, Sergeant. Use your blade well."

Zorro stopped short and surveyed the desperate fighting. "Where is Ruiz?" he shouted above the din.

Garcia shouted back. "Those devil pirates took him out to roast at the stake," he said. "It was long before the fighting and has surely been done." Then turning again to the battle he screamed, "Let me at these pirates. There are many scores to settle."

Zorro's heart sank. But a glimpse toward the center of the clearing gave him hope. Don Audre Ruiz, still alive, was indeed tied to a stake. And at his feet, snapping at him like living snakes, was a roaring fire. Zorro spun on his heels and bounded to his friend.

"Audre!" Zorro yelled. "If they have slain you—"

Don Audre Ruiz raised his head. His eyes, filled with smoke, saw his dear friend racing through the flames toward him.

In a second Zorro was at the stake. He kicked the roaring logs away from the helpless caballero's feet.

"You are just in time," Don Audre gasped. "I had given up hope, my friend."

"I'll have you free in a moment," Zorro said, tearing away the ropes and thongs. He struggled to break the chain, which in places was red hot. Now and then he glanced toward the battle to make certain he would not be taken by surprise. Finally, the chain fell away.

The two leaped from the roaring pyre. Zorro thrust a sword into his friend's hand. "Remember," he said. "Ramon belongs to me."

The caballeros raced to the edge of the fight. Zorro looked for Ramon, but the *comandante* was nowhere in sight.

"We must find him!" Zorro shouted. "He will be trying to get the señorita away."

Zorro and Don Audre Ruiz began a frantic search of the remaining buildings. They ran toward the beach, expecting to see the *comandante* riding away with the girl. But there was still no sign of the devious captain.

Sergeant Garcia was also looking for his captain. He was in a quandary. His commander was pitted against his friend. The sergeant could not be loyal to both. He fought his way through the battle, his eyes searching for Ramon.

Friar Felipe was tending to the wounded. As he leaned over one fallen man, a pirate raced by him in full flight. The man stumbled and a flash of light fell from his sash to the ground. It was the friar's sacred goblet!

The friar reached for the precious cup, but the pirate got it first.

"Give it to me," Friar Felipe demanded.

"I would be a fool to do so," the pirate retorted. He raised his cutlass to strike the frocked man down.

Suddenly the pirate's face twisted into a look of pain. His blade fell from his hand. He threw his arms wide and shrieking, dropped to the ground.

Sergeant Garcia stepped over the man and retrieved the goblet. He brushed it clean on his tunic and handed it to the grateful friar with a low bow. "It is a fortunate thing I was near, Friar," he said.

"I thank thee, son," the friar said.

The sergeant's grizzled face lighted up. "You call me son?" he asked with astonishment. "An old sinner like me?"

The friar smiled. "Perhaps you are worth more than you allow yourself to think," he said.

Sergeant Garcia's face grew red. He gulped loudly. "I am just a rough soldier," he said. "And I belong in this battle, which is almost at its end." He turned from the friar and with his head held high, charged through the smoke back to the thick of things.

Zorro's unexpected appearance at the battle when he was supposed to be a prisoner at the presidio of San Diego de Alcalá terrified Captain Ramon. He sensed the fates were against him and his treachery would soon be punished. Once again his plans were in ruin.

Ramon wished no personal encounter with Zorro. He knew such a meeting would not be in his favor. There was little chance he could now convince anyone Zorro was a traitor, while the odds were great that Zorro and some of the captured pirates could easily prove him to be one.

Ramon was desperate. He decided to find the señorita and ride away with her before the battle was over. Later, he could say that he thought the pirates were winning and he was only trying to save the young girl.

What he would do if he succeeded in getting the girl away from the camp, the treacherous captain did not know. He thought he might force her to wed him. He could become a highwayman and rob for a living. If she refused, he could abandon the girl and return among honest people claiming he knew nothing of her fate. Ramon's devious mind produced an endless number of schemes, each more grim than the last.

The captain finally found his way through the smoke and fire to the building holding the señorita. Once there he tied his horse nearby and crouched beside a low window.

The señorita sat inside, her face in her hands. A guard lounged near the door. The *comandante* drew his blade. When the raging battle behind him quieted for an instant, he shouted very loudly so the guard would be sure to hear. "Attack!" he screamed.

Thinking the battle was drawing near, the pirate opened the door. Ramon dropped him with a quick blow and entered the building.

The señorita sprang to her feet.

"Quick!" Ramon shouted to the young girl. "There is little time. The pirates are winning—"

But Lolita Pulido did not budge. "I am safer with them than with you," she said coldly.

Ramon grabbed her by the wrist. "Come with me," he commanded. "You cannot stop me with words."

The captain lifted the struggling girl and carried her to his horse where he placed her in the saddle.

"Help!" Lolita cried. "Zorro! Save me!"

Ramon laughed. "Call all you want, but this time it is too late."

But Zorro did hear. He saw the *comandante* leap atop the horse with Lolita and kick frantically at the horse's ribs.

And Ramon saw Zorro. He drove the terrified horse through the smoke.

Zorro's rage gave him great strength. He ran to Toranado who nervously pawed the ground and leaped onto the creature's back, turning him toward the fleeing captain.

The captain's horse emerged from a pall of smoke and struggled up the slope with its two riders clinging to its back. The grade was too steep, and the horse turned back to the clearing, riding full gallop toward Zorro.

The last thing Captain Ramon wanted was a face-to-face clash with the bold caballero who had bested him in every meeting. He guided the horse into the smoke, thinking he could lose his hot-blooded pursuer, but the turn only took him into the thick of the battle again.

Ramon was in a panic. He kicked fiercely at the horse's flanks with his spurs, but the frightened beast refused to move. A ring of caballeros circled the horse, and two of them grabbed the horse's reins. Ready hands helped the señorita to the ground while others grabbed for Ramon.

Zorro stopped a few feet from the terrified captain. "Down, traitor!" he commanded.

Though inwardly Ramon was panicked, outwardly he appeared calm. Sneering at his captors, he slowly climbed from the saddle.

The fighting was over. The pirates were captured. Bardoso himself was a prisoner. The lieutenant and his troopers rode toward Ramon and the caballeros.

"Here is Señor Zorro!" Ramon shouted at the lieutenant. "Seize him before he escapes again."

The lieutenant gave a command and several troopers dismounted. They moved forward only to find themselves stopped by the line of determined caballeros with drawn swords.

Don Audre Ruiz bowed to the young officer. "Señor," he said, "I do not like to interfere with the duties of an officer, but I must ask your men to stand back. There is a matter to be settled between Zorro and Captain Ramon."

"I am in command here under Captain Ramon," the lieutenant said. "This Señor Zorro is an escaped prisoner."

"Perhaps," Don Audre Ruiz said. "But you must remain quiet until the affair is ended. We caballeros do not recommend another fight."

"You are taking up arms against the governor," the puzzled lieutenant said.

Don Audre's voice was calm. "Ramon is a renegade and a traitor."

A loud voice arose from the crowd of pirate prisoners. "It is true," Bardoso shouted. "He joined hands with us and planned the raid against Reina de los Angeles so we could steal the señorita for him. Then he turned against us with a trap. Captain Ramon is a traitor."

Don Audre raised his voice. "These gentlemen whose honor and names are unquestioned will be responsible if a mistake is being made here, and they will take the consequences," he said. The caballeros all raised their swords in agreement.

The lieutenant didn't know what to do.

"Arrest this Señor Zorro," Captain Ramon ordered. "Do not listen to these meddlers—"

Zorro slapped Ramon's cheek with the flat of his hand. "On guard, murderous traitor," he said. "Prepare to fight."

Captain Ramon felt like a trapped animal. "Sergeant Garcia!" he called. "Arrest that man."

Garcia did not move. "I do not take commands from traitors," he said.

"I'll have you punished," Ramon shrieked.

"'Tis you who'll be punished when you lift your blade against Señor Zorro," the sergeant said.

Don Audre turned the señorita over to Friar Felipe. The hearty friar knew there was nothing he could do to stop the duel.

"On guard, señor," Zorro warned again.

Captain Ramon's sword hand quivered. He was white with terror, knowing that he faced sure defeat. He gulped, then raised his trembling sword.

Zorro's flashing sword scored the air so it sizzled. The hapless captain stared numbly at the blurred tip, which flew past his nose like an angry bee. It was a hopeless match and he knew it. Before he could react, Zorro delicately flicked his wrist and the deed was done. Ramon fell back, a fresh mark of Zorro emblazoned on his forehead atop the one already there.

But Zorro's anger was not yet spent. He advanced on the devious captain, stinging him again and again with his keen blade. Ramon slashed back as if flailing with a heavy stick. His spirit was completely broken. A flurry of thrusts by Zorro's sword cut away the buttons of his tunic one by one. Another opened his shirt and still another slashed away the thick leather belt holding up his trousers. "Enough!" the traitorous captain screamed as he struggled to keep his pants on.

Zorro grinned. He held nothing but contempt for this man who now stood before him as helpless as a swordsman's practice dummy. With a lunge his sword struck again. An epaulet of Captain Ramon's rank flew from his shoulder.

"That for your deeds against the people," Zorro exclaimed.

He struck a final time. The other epaulet fell to the ground. The once powerful officer was reduced to nothing more than the cringing coward he'd always been. "And that for your crimes against my friends and the young señorita I have sworn to protect."

Ramon, Bardoso, and the pirate band were herded into the adobe hut that had lately held the caballeros prisoner. Their treachery would be amply punished.

Zorro raised his sword. "To our victory," he shouted to his men.

"To Zorro!" they cried, their swords raised in salute. "Protector of justice. Zorro!"

That night the moon rose over the silver sea once again. The trading schooner plied the waves, her crew aided by the caballeros, heading up the coast and away from the terrible scene of battle.

Friar Felipe sat near the bow polishing his beloved goblet. Don Audre Ruiz was tending his injured comrades in the cabins below. And big Sergeant Garcia wandered aimlessly about the deck, his soldier's boots on uncertain pinning.

Garcia stopped at the rail and gazed toward the dark strip of land in the distance. On a bluff overlooking the sea, lighted from behind by a bright moon, rode the silhouette of a man in a flowing black cape atop a valiant black steed. A silver sword glistened in his upraised hand. The horse reared at its rider's command. A booming voice drifted over the waves to the ship.

"*Atención*! A caballero's near . . . !" it rang out.

Another voice captured the sergeant's rapt attention. It came from the shadows where another figure watched the bold horseman from the ship and listened to his song.

Señorita Lolita Pulido, her heart beating rapidly, put her fingers to her lips and blew an unseen kiss to the masked caballero. "Oh, Zorro," she said softly. "If only you knew my secret love for you." She raised her face to the moon, which cast its soft light on her and her secret love. "Perhaps some day we can be together—" Her voice trailed off into silence. It was too soon to know what the future might hold.

Friar Felipe joined Sergeant Garcia at the rail. The friends watched as Zorro rode out of sight. "Let us hope the sword of Zorro can now be put to rest," he said.

The sergeant rubbed his ruddy jowls. "Perhaps," he said with a certain wisdom that surprised even him. "But as long as men are men, we can only hope and see. Yet I for one would not be surprised to hear that voice again when justice calls. . . ."

And as the good sergeant spoke, the echo of a stirring refrain drifted over the waves as a sign.

"*Atención*! A caballero's near. . . ."